LILY'S MISTAKE

Also by Pamela Ann

Chasing Beautiful

Chasing Imperfection

Scornfully Yours

LILY'S MISTAKE

By: Pamela Ann

LILY'S MISTAKE

ACKNOWLEDGMENTS

I just want to thank my beta readers, Tia Marie, Dawn Martens and Cami Hesnault for being so awesome! This novel wouldn't be the same without you guys.

To my family, thank you for everything.

To my two white puffy puffballs, Sugar and Cookie, thank you for staying up late and keeping me company.

For my mom,

Thank you for being amazing.

PROLOGUE

Eighteen Years Ago

Lily

"Are you ready yet?" I call out from the bush I'm hiding behind. I don't want Drake to get a peek at me while I'm getting ready.

"All set!"

I'm a few yards away from the white gazebo. Fixing my wildflower crown, I stand and slowly walk towards Drake's line of sight. My hands tighten around the assortment of flowers bundled in my hands, but my shakiness vanishes when my eyes meet Drake's. He's gazing at me sheepishly as he waits for my approach.

I fight the urge to just run up to him; I know I shouldn't, though. Weddings are supposed to be savored. Fairytales are forever and I have all the time in the world to get there.

I reach the few steps of the gazebo and almost falter going up them when Drake whispers, "You look beautiful."

I give him a toothy smile in return.

We are finally standing side by side when he asks, "How do we do this? Do we just say forever and ever, then that's it?"

"Gosh, I don't know. How did they do it at your cousin's wedding yesterday?"

Drake bites his lips as he thinks it through. "I don't remember much, but I can try, I guess."

"Good."

He clears his throat and speaks, "I, Drake Tatum, take Lily Alexander forever and a day. I promise to give her flowers and kisses forever and ever until I die." I giggle when Drake mentions kisses. "It's your turn now, Lil. Just follow what I said."

I nod and clear my throat. Smiling, I repeat his words. "I, Lily Alexander, take Drake forever. I promise to give him kisses and share my Reese's peanut buttercups once a week forever and ever until I die."

"That was not what I said, Lil! Now you just ruined it!"

I giggle again. "Drake! Just stop it. Aren't you supposed to kiss me now?" He suddenly looks nervous.

"I guess"

When I see his face closing in on mine, I close my eyes and wait for his kiss. I catch my breath as his lips touch mine. It's short and sweet, but it seals my fate; I will forever be Drake's girl.

When I open my eyes and blink a few times, I see Drake grinning at me. "There! Now we're married!"

"Kids! Wedding's over! It's snack time," his mother, Patricia, interrupts us.

When we pass by her, she laughs at our silliness. Once she piles our plates with sandwiches and cookies, she looks amusedly back at us. "So, how does it feel to be married?"

"I love it!" I exclaim.

1

"Hello?"

"How did your job interview go honey?" my mother's soft voice asks on the other end of the phone. "It looks promising. They said they'll call me in two weeks." I maneuver my car out of the parking lot.

I've been job hunting for the last three months with no prospects at all. I got fired from my last secretarial job when Mrs. Donald caught Mr. Donald trying to seduce me. Allan Donald is a true gentleman, That is, he was before his usual cocktail concoction of gin and brandy for breakfast. Then he became a little *comfortable*. It wasn't the first time I had slapped his hand away, but this time, Carla Donald was there to witness it and fired me on the spot.

"I called because Patricia's back in town and wants you to join us for lunch at The Four Seasons."

Patricia Tatum is my godmother as well as my mother's best friend since they were in diapers. She married Hugh Tatum, a very well-known import/export business man who is also a major financial backer for Hollywood blockbuster films.

"What time? It's almost noon." I glance back at the clock on the dashboard.

"Well, yes, dear, we need you to meet us right now." My mom sounds a tad urgent.

"Sure. See you in a bit." It's almost lunchtime and my stomach growls.

A simple lunch at The Four Seasons would just be super!

What could possibly go wrong?

======

My appetite, apparently, as my godmother announces the reason behind this sudden lunch date.

I blink a few times, taken aback from what has just spouted off her rouge-tinted lips. "Excuse me? Did you just say Drake's thinking of marriage?" I look at Patricia like she's just offended me.

Well, I suppose anything that involves Drake I would find offensive. Good or bad.

"Yes, and to a monstrous, gold-digging, horrible woman!" Patricia dabs the sides of her eyes. The woman was a complete mess when I joined them five minutes prior and she has only slightly calmed in the time since.

Her words sink in, slowly and start gnawing inside me. Drake Tatum's planning on marriage? No shit?

I don't know if I should be happy or cry a freaking dam of tears to that news. Drake Tatum used to be the center of my universe. He was my first love and the first man I ever made love to, as well as the very same man who walked away like I was diseased the very day after he took my virginity.

Drake's two years older than me, which means he's now engaged at the age of twenty-eight. Isn't that a bit early for a well-known "man whore" to marry?

Oh yeah, Drake's long line of women are quite known around Hollywood. He dates up and coming actresses, models, musicians and so forth, his notoriety is legendary. He's working alongside his father. After spending a lot of his time studying in Columbia, then staying around New York after he graduated, he comes to Los Angeles periodically from what I've gathered from my mother and Patricia. Not to mention, what I know from Google. I couldn't help searching for the man every once in a while.

"Would that work for you, dear?" my mom, Hope, asks. Both women looked at me like I had the answer for salvation.

"Huh? Sorry my mind went off somewhere." Yeah, somewhere that shouldn't have Drake in it. He's the epitome of a player: an insensitive jerk and a two-timing prick to boot! The absolute worst of the worst.

"I was asking if you would be Drake's personal assistant for a while. His recent one just quit because his fiancée, Shannon, drove the poor girl crazy."

HUH?

"Me? I don't want to work with Drake. He and I hate each other for crying out loud!" Everybody knows it. I haven't even laid eyes on him since I was eighteen, and I want to keep it that way.

"Please, Lily, my son's future is on the line here. All I need for you to do is report to me about Shannon and make her a little jealous." Patricia stops me before I can object. "I've met her and she's nothing but fake. I know you and Drake don't get along; however, please, can't you do this? Hugh and I are desperate here."

"Even Hugh hates her?" How is that possible? Hugh loves everyone, as long as they're not against him in the business arena; he's all hugs and kisses.

Patricia nods. "Will you do this for us, honey? You're like a daughter to me, Lil. I would appreciate it if you could lend us a hand."

Man, she used the "you're like my daughter" line. How can I say no to that? If I ever had a second mom, it would be Patricia. I did grow up with them treating me like I was their own. Hugh and my father became close over the years as well. My father's death when I was seventeen only made our bond with the Tatum's even stronger.

I finally concede. "Okay, I'll do it for you and Hugh."

Patricia gets up and hugs me. "Thank you, Lil! I knew I could count on you!" She kisses my forehead and squeezes my hand before going back to her chair.

"Now all you have to do is try not to kill each other before fixing this problem with Shannon, hmmm?" My mother quirks her dark eyebrows at me.

"We shall see," I murmur.

I spend another hour with them, but skip the spa ritual that Patricia and Mom always indulge in after lunch; wanting to be alone. They do this once or twice a week and won't miss me, anyway. My thoughts keep wandering around Drake; ever since Patricia mentioned him, I have been having a hard time getting him off my mind. Drake and I grew up together. We were inseparable. I worshipped the ground that he walked on from about the age of eight, I think. I suppose I loved him so much that I didn't see any of his flaws back then. Even at that young age, Drake was already a handsome kid. His clear, grey eyes never failed to capture and hold me in a trance.

Everything changed the summer after I turned eighteen, though.

2

Eight Years Ago . . .

Playa del Carmen, México

"Are you two sure that it'll be okay for us to stay overnight in Cozumel without you?" Hugh asks both Drake and me.

"I don't mind staying here; I want to go to the beach party tonight." I smile at Hugh and Patricia.

I met this guy, Ricardo, last night at the local bar. He invited me to a beach party tonight and I'm so going. Drake was always talking on the phone to his new girlfriend, anyway; he's been ignoring me mostly the entire time. We've been here for four days and he's only asked me to swim with him once. ONCE!

Back in the day, he and I used to do everything together. I guess Columbia University changed him.

"We're good here, Mom and Dad. You guys have fun!" Drake hugs each of his parents and they kiss him back before waving goodbye.

I miss my dad at the oddest times. It used to be all six of us vacationing here, but now it's just four of us. Mom decided at the last minute to join her friend in Paris for a whole month. It's only been a little over a year since my dad's passing, but I still miss him like mad. I guess this hole in my life will stay there forever and I will never be quite the same.

I bite my lip and start to walk towards the kitchen when Drake speaks, "You're going alone to a beach party tonight?"

Oh, now he's talking to me? "No. I have a date. In fact, he's picking me at four, so that leaves me another hour," I announce over my shoulder and continue walking towards the kitchen.

I get a mango from the fruit bowl on the granite kitchen counter and grab a knife when Drake joins me, sitting on the counter next to the chopping board.

"Who's your date?" I can feel his eyes following me.

Why the sudden concern?

Peeling off the mango skin with quick ease, I immediately chop it in half before I respond, "His name's Ricardo, why?"

"I don't want you going on dates, Lil. You're too innocent for those things." He takes a piece of mango and pops it into his lush mouth.

My eyes are glued to his pink lips. His Adam's apple bobs and I begin to study his masculine neck. Everything about him is completely masculine, truly sexy. And that hot, handsome face, where do I begin with that? I want him so bad, but he never notices me that way. I guess I'm not pretty or sexy enough for him.

Well, I'm tired of waiting for him to come to his senses, anyway.

Yeah, I've been waiting! It's obvious to anyone with eyes that I adore and love Drake. I've declined each guy who asked me out all through high school because there was never a doubt in my mind that I'll only ever want Drake. To me, no one else comes close. I even had enough balls to throw myself at him during New Year's Eve, but he pushed me off.

"Stop drinking, Lily. Being a slut doesn't suit you." Said by the very man, himself, when he rejected me.

Too bad! Tonight, I will let loose.

Tonight, I'm finally getting rid of my virginity; thank you very much. The chosen man is the hot Brazilian, Ricardo Belmonte!

I shrug. "Not for long, I won't!" I saunter in my hot pink, bikini clad body towards the open patio doors, sit on one of the cushioned loungers and enjoy the view with my mangoes.

"Hold on, Lily. You can't be serious, right? You barely know this Ricardo dude! You can't just do that!" Drake sits across from me only wearing his surfer shorts.

He doesn't even bother checking out my almost naked body. See what I mean? He's immune to me. I shrug, hurt. Whatever, life moves on.

I try to train my eyes away from those perfect washboard abs and those metallic grey eyes. Why does he have to be so fucking hot??? His dirty blonde hair even has that sexy out-of-the-bed look. I guess it's just my luck that I had to grow up with the most handsome guy I have ever laid eyes on. A guy who doesn't clearly feel the same about me, but I've decided to start living. Eighteen is the start of self-discovery and I plan to do just that.

"Whatever, Drake. Is that all?" I take a bite from a mango slice and lick my fingers. *I love me some mangoes,* I think happily.

"No, it's not ALL. It's a stupid idea, Lil. You're not stupid, so don't do stupid things that you will soon regret."

I sit up from the lounger and face him. "You're one to talk! What's your problem anyway? Now you're talking to me? You think I haven't noticed how you've tried to ignore me the entire time we've been here? I'm not an idiot, Drake. I told you I was sorry about what happened during New Year's, but for some reason, you still feel weird about it." I screech. When I glance at him, his eyes are on my breasts, but he immediately drags them away and stares at the sea instead. Sigh.

"This is not about New Year's, Lil. You know what? Do whatever you want!" He sounds angry as he gets up, leaving for the beach. His well sculpted back and bottom are even gorgeous!

Great! I really need to get over it!

It's high time Drake Tatum moves out of my mind and hopefully out of my heart.

======

"You look very beautiful, Lily, mi belleza!" Ricardo purrs. We are at the restaurant we agreed to meet up at. The party is close by and he wants us to grab something to eat before partying it up.

"Gracias, Ricardo." I kiss his tanned cheek. He leads us inside the restaurant where we are immediately escorted by the hostess to a table overlooking the breathtakingly beautiful Caribbean Sea.

I don't consider myself in the 'knockout' department, but some guys find me appealing. I'm five-seven, have long, dark brown hair, amber/hazel eyes, but I'm quite lacking in the breast department with my B-cups. The only redeemable asset I have is my perky bottom. My lithe, toned body is thanks to my night time swim routine and my dedication to Pilates.

We hit the beach party right around six and the sun is setting beautifully in the backdrop. Spanish raggaeton music is blaring loud on the speakers. I have already had two strawberry margaritas and am loving the carefree beach ambiance.

Ricardo and I go over to the bar and he orders four shots of Patron.

"To mi belleza and to your beautiful vacation in Mexico!" Ricardo holds up his shot glass.

"Cheers, Ricky Ricardo!" I hoot back and take the shots back to back. The Patron burns smoothly as it goes down my throat and into my stomach. "Ahh!" I shiver.

"Come on, time to party!"

Ricardo hugs my hips as we grind to the music. I'm pretty much plastered, but I don't care much because I'm letting go and finally having fun!

I giggle when Ricardo's lips find the back of my ear. "You smell good, Belleza."

"GET YOUR HANDS OFF HER!" Drake yanks me off Ricardo in an instant. I blink a few times. My hazy, drunk-filled state confuses me for a second.

"Drake!"

"Hey! She's my girl. Go look for a different one to tango with, no? She's mine!" a drunken Ricky Ricardo says.

"Lily's always been mine."

"Mierda!" Ricardo cusses before he leaves for the bar.

"Hey!" I call out to him, but Drake drags me away from the party and stomps up the shoreline that leads to the villa. It's half a mile away and I'll be damned if I'm walking that far drunk.

"What the FUCK Drake! I'm going back to the party!" I try to detach my arm from his tight hold, but he holds me closer.

"Let me go, Drake!"

"Don't fight me off Lily. You're drunk!" We stop walking as he glares at me with those steel eyes. Shit, the moonlight makes him look like a dark, hot... sexy panther.

Earth to Lily, hello? I swallow. Get a grip Lil, seriously!

"What are you doing, Drake?" I whisper to him, searching the depths of his ice grey eyes.

"We'll talk about it once we get to the villa," he says, turning on his heel and starting to walk again.

I look back at the party and realize that we've been walking for quite some time now. In the distance, the beach is alight with the full moon. I stop to take in the scene and try to calm my hammering heart. Why is Drake acting out of character? He's never acted this way.

Maybe he realizes he loves me after all? Fat chance... but what if that is it?

"Drake, stop."

"What?" he asks over his shoulder, but doesn't stop to gaze at the beautiful moonlit sea.

I'm unsure of how to broach the subject, but it's now or never. It's just him and me out here tonight. Surely he's not going to push me away?

"Why are you acting like a jealous boyfriend? I thought you said you weren't interested . . ." I bite my lip as I see him stomp towards me. His chiseled body looks even more appealing with the moonlight highlighting the planes of his body and his eyes are a smoldering, liquid silver.

My body starts to tremor just looking at the handsome creature before me. His face is masked with something I can't quite figure out, it's intense and forbidding. We stand there for a good minute, staring at each other. Wondering what the fuck is going on. "Drake . . ."

"You shouldn't want a man like me, Lil. I'm not good enough for you." Drake sounds serious; however, I'm having none of it.

No . . . You're even better . . . I've never met anyone like you. The rest of the men lack brilliance when compared to you . . .

"Why would you say that? You're the only one I want." I move closer, feeling brazen when he doesn't move away. I stand on my tiptoes and lick his lips. He tastes of salt and something masculine. My heart is beating erratically; I feel exhilarated and faint at the same time from being so close to him. "I want you . . . I want you to be the one to take my virginity away."

I feel Drake's chest heave before he rasps out, "I don't think you get what I'm trying to tell you here . . ."

Yes, I'm not dense, but I want you so much, Drake Tatum. I've loved you for so long. Tonight, I will have you . . . even for a little while.

"I do, but would you rather I do it with someone else then, like Ricardo, perhaps?" I know I'm playing with fire . . . but I'm desperate. I want Drake to see me as a woman. A woman he can be with and desire—not the little girl with frilly dresses that would follow him around.

"Don't even go there, Lil," he resigns, heavily huffing and continues on, "OKAY, if this is what you want, then meet me on the veranda in fifteen minutes. Go get ready because there will be no backing out once you come to me. Think it through, okay?"

What else was there to think through? It's what I've wanted; what I've waited for.

3

Present

Drake shows me the world that night as he takes me underneath the stars on the patio bed.

The next day I realize that world has two sides. One world of ceaseless ecstasy and one full of crumbled, guttered and wretched pain from having your love thrown back at you.

Yes, Drake Tatum irrevocably broke my heart and I will never, ever forget it.

"I will be upstairs, Dear," Patricia Tatum says.

It's a quarter before nine and she is being kind enough to guide me on my first day of work in Tatum Worldwide, Inc. I suppose she needed to make sure that I will really go through with her plans.

"Okay, I'm coming into the parking lot now. Be up soon," I respond before cutting off the call.

I'm a nervous wreck. I've been up since five this morning and already had two cups of coffee. I skipped on breakfast because I didn't think I could keep anything down, but who could blame me? I haven't seen Drake in eight years—eight long years after that fiasco in Mexico. I did wait around for him, even going overboard by trying to visit him at Colombia, but he emailed me stating that he was with someone and wouldn't appreciate my intrusion. After his rebuff, I finally realized what little I meant to him; if I ever meant anything to him at all.

I'm dressed in a fitted black skirt suit and my favorite black pumps. I need to look professional and still pull-off the slick and sexy look. Heck, yes! Given the circumstances, I will not go in there looking drab and dowdy, my pride won't allow it.

Once inside the large marbled building, I immediately seek the reception desk. They have already been informed about me and have my security pass ready.

I smirk when I see my picture was actually taken two years ago. I'm sure she got that from my mother. Patricia Tatum really is adamant about booting the woman in her son's life. I guess the mother-in-laws really are the ones to watch out for, right?

Following what I've been instructed to do, I dart towards a separate private elevator. My security card is cleared for all levels; however, this elevator goes straight to the top floor. I've been informed that the top floor houses only Drake's and Hugh's offices.

As I step out, I can see that the offices are decorated in all glass and white walls; everything looks crisp and pristine. The black marbled floor is so shiny, I'm sure I could use it as a mirror.

"Miss Lily Alexander? Hello, I'm Suzy Summers, the floor receptionist." A smiling petite blonde rushes towards me and holds out a hand.

"Hello, Suzy. How do you do?" I smile back, taking her outstretched hand and shaking it.

"I'm awesome. Mrs. Hugh is in Mr. Drake's office. She's been waiting for you. You can go through those large doors on the left and Mindy, his secretary, will be there to assist you further." I graciously thank her and head towards the direction she gave me.

When I go through the doors, I'm surprised Mindy isn't there. It's a large room with two large desks and another reception area in the corner. Another set of heavy doors are located on the far end and I rush towards them. I gently knock and push it forward.

Patricia is sitting idly on the white couch, looking bored while drinking her morning coffee and eating a few pastries. She looks up when she sees me.

"Good morning, my dear." She strides forward and gives me a tight motherly hug. "Thank you, again, for doing this favor for us." Patricia holds my chin and smiles beautifully at me.

"No problem. It's not like I can say no to my godmother and Hugh anyway." I kiss her cheek, go to the couch and sit down.

The cute, bite-size pastries look delicious and I pick one out. Patricia heads over to prepare another cup of coffee.

I sigh when she hands it to me. "Thank you, Pat," I murmur.

"Soooo," Patricia says as she sits next to me, "Drake should be here soon, but I think I should be here just in case he rejects the idea and you two end up fighting."

I guess we're that predictable?

I nod as I take a sip of coffee. "Are you seeing anyone, Lil? Your mom says you aren't, but a pretty young lady like you would have a busy schedule, right?" Patricia leans back and studies me.

After the demise of my close relationship with Drake, I eventually started to withdraw from being around his family, too. It's just too hard and it's easier to ignore everyone that is related to him. It's childish, I know, but it is the best I can do and eight years on, it's a habit I can't break. Although I see them once every few months, I avoid any parties and events that Drake attends. I guess I'm now realizing it's time to bury the hatchet and move on. I can't hold a grudge forever, now can I?

"I actually just started dating someone. His name is Jared Johnson. Nothing serious, yet, we're still in the 'getting to know you' stage. Why? Has mom said something?" Mom is always trying to set me up on dates. She feels like I should start working on her grandchild very soon. Seriously, I'm only twenty-six, what's the rush?

"I was curious is all—" We are interrupted by the sudden opening of the door.

Drake comes in, dressed casually in a pair of rugged jeans and a white dress shirt with his sleeves rolled up. *Wow, scruffy and very sexy indeed!* I think with piqued interest. Time has only made him look better. Gone is the boyish look and in its place is definitely a man. A man with a dangerous appeal and tons of charisma.

"No, baby. I'm already at work—" He cuts off mid-sentence when he sees that he has visitors.

With his eyes glued on me, he instantly cuts his call short. "Lemme call you back."

Silver, glittering eyes penetrate me like laser beams. "Well, well, well. This is a nice surprise on a Monday morning, Mother, Lily. How may I assist you both?" He goes over to Patricia's side and kisses her cheek.

Drake then sits on the chaise sofa opposite us; metallic eyes still glued on me. I should be intimidated by those gorgeous eyes and their intensity, but I'm simply not. In fact, it has the opposite effect. I feel revitalized and enlivened. Something shifts inside me. It's something that I cannot pinpoint at this very moment, but I know it has a purpose.

Could it be closure? That I'm not the love struck, sick puppy to this man anymore? Quite possibly . . . it's somewhere along the lines of that. It just has to be.

"I hired Lily as your new assistant. We were just catching up. How's your morning, my dear son?" Patricia looks at Drake with an expression full of love and affection. It's no secret how Hugh and Pat adore their only child. They wanted to have another baby, but Patricia couldn't get pregnant anymore. I suppose, maybe, that's why she dotes on me. Even if I don't see her much, each week she will send muffins, flowers, chocolates or whatever else she can think of. She's a sweetheart and loves me like her own daughter.

"I see. I actually requested HR to start interviewing for that position." He leans over and gets himself a croissant. I notice how big and manly his hand is; it's quite sexy.

Shit, do I have to associate sexy with him all the time? Get a grip, Lil!

"Oh, your father already took care of that the instant Lily agreed to work for you." She places her coffee down on the mahogany table.

Drake momentarily stills. "I see."

Does he really SEE?

He clears his throat and gets up. "I suppose that's a done deal. You okay with that, Lil?" His silver eyes land on me, again.

I give him a cat-like smile. "Oh, yeah, I sure am." Hell yeah, I am. I'm going to enjoy torturing the jackass. Bury the hatchet, my ass! I guess my evil side is starting to come out? I can really see myself having a little fun making his life a little difficult. Yes, that definitely sounds enticing.

"That's lovely! It's great to see you two in the same room again. It's been a long time, hasn't it? Since Mexico, I mean," Patricia wonders.

Oh crapper, did she have to bring up that subject? What happened in Mexico with Drake was a mistake. Drake was a mistake.

"Uh-huh . . ." I respond, reaching for my coffee again. I need some kind of distraction.

Patricia stands up and gathers her purse. "Alright, children, I'll leave you two to hash the details out. I have to get ready to meet your mother for our tennis match." She kisses me, then Drake before striding out the door with gracious composure. She can be intimidating, especially when she's all riled up, but Patricia is still a stunning woman.

With only the two of us in his office, it just starts to get awkward. *Time to get moving,* I think with enthusiasm.

"So, will you show me my office and we can go over the details of my job?" I look up to him innocently, quite ready to start working. This job is a great opportunity for me to meet new people and gain new connections. Maybe even meet a few guys along the way.

"You're really serious about this? Mom didn't force you to work for me? Maybe spy on me a little on the side?" Drake quirks up a brow.

Ha.

I shrug. "Your mom said you needed an assistant. I needed a job." It's not technically a lie. I just danced around his questions a bit.

4

"Right." Drake is still studying me like a specimen for some kind of exhibit.

I stand up and skim my hands over my skirt, smoothing out the invisible wrinkles. "Okay. Can we now get started?" I go to grab my purse; not wanting to talk to Drake any more than I have to.

"I haven't seen you in eight years, Lil. Is that all you have to say? There's no 'How are you, Drake?' or 'It's nice to see you again?'"

Uh, not really.

We didn't really part on good terms, so I see no need for pleasantries or the pretense that it *is* nice to see him because I could care less about how he's doing—or who he's doing, for that matter.

"To be honest, I don't really care for that," I admit. "I came here to work for you and that's what I'll do. We're not friends anymore, Drake," I state it as matter-of-factly as possible.

"You're right. We were just practically like family. We were never friends." His hand goes to the side of his scruffy jaw, rubbing along it. I can tell he's still waiting and stalling with this conversation.

Why can't he just drop it? It was a long, long time ago.

"Yep!" I look at him as he leans over his desk, looking confused. "So... can we move on from that and get to work?"

He folds his arms and is silent for a good minute. I guess he can't really drop it, huh?

"Have you really moved on from it, Lily?" His heavily loaded question hits me like a ton of bricks.

Whoa, WTF!

"Whatever do you mean?" I ask innocently. Is he actually this dense? Can't he simply understand that I don't want to rehash and chitchat about the damn past?

"You've been avoiding me. Why is that? Both of our mothers are like sisters, and yet, I haven't seen you in almost a decade. Now, out of the blue, my mom decides to hire you as my assistant. Isn't that a little sketchy, perhaps even fishy to you?"

"No, I don't think so. I haven't been avoiding you. I just couldn't stomach seeing you again." *Oops, isn't that the same thing?* "After Mexico, I realized I made a mistake. *You* were a huge mistake. So, there. There is your reason." I hold my head high as I speak those words to him.

He means nothing to me. Not anymore.

"A mistake . . . Right. You didn't seem to mind it when I was taking your virginity. To which, I recall, you freely gave away for any man who was willing."

JACKASS!

I grind my teeth together and gather all the energy I can muster from the universe to compose myself and not shriek with rage. "Sure, that night was okay." I shrug. "It was meh . . . nothing earth-shattering now that I've had better." *Ha! Shove it, you douche,* I think.

My words clearly affect him. Men and their sexual prowess . . . all you have to do is question it and they go mental.

"I see. You've developed quite a tongue there, Lil. You better tame your temper if you don't want a repeat of 'nothing earth-shattering' sex." I blanch at his sexual innuendo. Has he lost his marbles?

"Trust me, I'd rather train a tiger than get to tumble in the sheets with you; thank you very much." I walk towards the door with my purse in hand and look back at the confusing, sexy man. "If you're still hell bent about the past, stay here and ponder some more, okay? I'll find my desk and figure it out on my own since my boss is too caught up in his own thoughts." His facial expression is simply priceless as I open the door and slam it hard behind me . . .

I smugly congratulate myself for not making a huge deal and a bigger fool out of myself after seeing him again. True, I may have loved the man to distraction back in yesteryears, but that ship has sailed. He doesn't get to take my virginity and simply walk away like it doesn't matter, like I didn't matter. His vicious rejection scarred me forever and it will forever be ingrained in my head; I would be stupid to forget it.

Once you give up your heart to the man you love, it ultimately gives them power. I've been stupid enough to succumb to his easy charm before. Never again, Drake Tatum, never fucking again.

I glance at Mindy's office, but she still isn't in there. Where is she?

There is another office next to Mindy's and I go open it. To my relief, it's empty except for the computer that sits on the desk. The office is small, but clean and has an airy feel to it. I suppose all the glass that surrounds it makes it less claustrophobic. The contrast between the black carpet and the white office furniture combines to make it sleek and chic. I love this office. I can easily picture myself working here. *But do you really want to work for Drake?* The voice in my head counters. Who knows? The man might be insufferable, yet, maybe as a boss, he won't be so bad. Just as long as he knows the boundaries and doesn't cross the line, then it won't be a problem.

I stride inside and immediately start working. I turn on the computer and place my purse in my desk drawer. Since I don't have any office supplies, I seek out the supply room. It's easily found because the room has a 'Supply Room' nameplate on the oak door.

Unknowingly, I start to whistle, but stop when I hear mewling sounds and sobs coming from somewhere in the room. I pursue the sounds to find out who they are coming from. I find a stylish, dressed to impress, black woman hunched over the copying machine, crying.

I tense. I guess she didn't hear me?

"Excuse me—are you alright? I don't mean to pry, but I heard you and I'm a little concerned," I whisper at the sullen woman's form. She immediately glances up when she hears me.

She sniffs again, trying to wipe the running mascara, but the hasty brush of her fingers makes it even worse. "Sorry. You must be the new girl. I'm Mindy." She sniffs once again.

Is she okay? She looks so distraught. I want to hug her, though I hold myself back just in case she thinks I'm a weirdo or something.

"I'm Lily Alexander. Are you okay, Mindy? Is there anything I can get you? Water, perhaps?"

"I'm a mess. Give me a second or two and then I'll be good as new," she states, yet I'm not convinced. Even in her state, it's obvious how pretty Mindy is, but I doubt her puffy eyes and nose will clear away that quickly.

I nod and smile at her. "Alright, but if you need someone to talk to, I'm here." Mindy nods and excuses herself to the restroom.

Confused from that little scene, I mentally shrug and seek out the supplies that I came here for in the first place.

I'm in the midst of putting some pens and pencils away in my office when I hear I light knock. I look up and find Mindy.

"Hey, come on in."

She strolls in with her tight, black slacks and fitted, engine red V-neck top. *Wow, what I would give to have a nice rack like hers*, I think annoyingly. Hers even look real—a commodity in Los Angeles. A lot of women here are enhanced and altered. Sad to say, but it's the damn truth.

Mindy sits on one of the white leather seats across from my desk. "You probably must've thought I was some loony, finding me crying in the supply closet like that, didn't you?" She chuckles. "I don't blame you. I didn't want to meet you in that state." She looks away for a second. "I need to learn how to separate my personal life and my work. I tend to mesh them together and it can be overwhelming sometimes."

"Don't worry about it. I get it—we're women. I can be emotional at times, too. You don't have to explain yourself to me."

Mindy flashes me a genuine, knockout smile. "Thank you. You know—I like you already. You have this aura around you; I find it very soothing and I feel like you really do mean what you say."

"Thank you. That's a very nice thing to say."

Mindy gets up and is about to leave my office when I speak again. "This might sound stupid, but can you tell me what I'm supposed to be doing right now?"

"Bring a notepad and go to Drake's office. He should direct you and tell you what he needs to be done." She turns around and then pauses, again. "Drake Tatum is a great man to work for. A little difficult at times, but he's fair and square. Try not to mind his fiancée, though. She's a class-A bitch, but other than that, it should be smooth sailing. See you in a bit." I give her a small smile and sit in my chair with a frustrated sigh.

Everyone always mentions this Shannon woman being so abhorrent. I would love to see this girlfriend of his. Or maybe I can easily just Google her and not wonder any longer.

Let me just finish going over Drake's calendar for today then I can freely quest about his infamous girlfriend, I think wickedly.

5

Clearing my throat, I make sure I have my notepad and pen in hand before I knock on Drake's office door. I push the heavy, oak door open and pause when he glances up from his laptop. For a second, his eyes flash an emotion for a split second before they become cold.

I lick my lips, trying to appear nonchalant. "I need to go over your schedule for today. I can't, for some reason, find your old agenda anywhere." My feet start working again and I advance to his desk and sit on one of the leather chairs, opposite him.

His eyes linger on me, tracing and caressing with cold assessment; they stay targeted on me in a quiet stare. Uncomfortable, I uncross and cross my legs and place the notepad on my lap. "Are you ready? Or do you want me to come back some other time?" I inquire lightly, trying in earnest not to melt under his heavy scrutiny.

Drake leans back in his chair and folds his arms, his muscles bulging beneath his shirt. "How have you been, Lil? And don't give me that crap of being okay. I want to know how you are and how life's been for you."

Taken aback by his question, I weigh my options. Should I counter his question with a smartass reply or answer it honestly like a civilized adult?

Common sense wins out. "I am doing mighty okay given the circumstances. Mom and I are fine, really, but I'm sure you know that already. So, why ask?"

"I just had to," he murmurs, then clears his throat. "We can go over my agenda now, if you'd like?"

I press my lips together, trying to figure out what's behind his odd attitude. Okay, I get that he's a little shocked seeing me again, I feel that way, too, but does he have to bring something about us up every time I walk in here? I've been here for a little over two hours and Drake's still talking about the time in between Mexico and now.

"I need you to make an appointment for me with Lavern O'Malley of Lights Studios. Make that a business lunch, anytime this week. After that's confirmed, I need you to make a restaurant reservation. Somewhere quiet so we can talk. Italian or American to be exact." I write down everything he has said.

Without looking up, I ask him. "Do you have a particular restaurant in mind?"

He shakes his head. "No. You can choose. Somewhere five-star if you get my drift." Obviously; like he'd dine anywhere else less, especially when he's on a business lunch.

"Order me a box of black Armani crew tees, large. You should have a company credit card issued under your name in the HR department, you can go get that and use it for the purchases."

"Send flowers to Cedars-Sinai Hospital for Christian Liberty. You can write a card along the lines of get well soon and such." I nod as I jot down his commands.

"I'm due for my physical and dental appointment. I need you to get on that. Also, get me two courtside tickets for the next Lakers' game. I need my dry-cleaning picked up and dropped off at my house in Malibu. My closet is color coordinated, so it shouldn't be too hard on you to figure out where it all goes. My dog, Skull, needs to be groomed."

I look up. "You have a dog?" I ask, astonished. He was never keen on dogs, ever.

"I do. Skull's been with me for about eight years now."

"Oh, but you hate dogs," I counter.

"Someone once told me that dogs can be the greatest of companions. They're loyal to their owners and will love you unconditionally." Is he for real? I told him that when I was sixteen and he was eighteen, playing a video game in my parents' living room. He just recited it verbatim.

"But, you hated dogs! You can't just like them because I told you they're great animals!"

"People change, Lil. You have, from what I can see."

"Riiiight . . ." I murmur, more than confused. "Will that be all?"

"Have lunch with me." Before I can decline his offer, he continues, "We can talk more about work while we eat." Okay, I guess if it's about work then I can do it.

"When do you want to leave?"

"I need to make a quick call, and then I'll come and get you." Drake delivers the words with finality.

I give him a quick nod and walk out of his office.

To be quite honest, I'm edgy where Drake's concerned. I can't read him—well I never really could—the man is an enigma. It's baffling how he could grow up so guarded. Patricia and Hugh are the greatest of parents and the only people I know that Drake freely shows affection to—well, and my mom, of course.

When I'm back in my new office, I do the first task on my notepad. Mindy is kind enough to send me all of Drake's contacts. I call Lavern O'Malley's office and speak to her assistant, setting up the business lunch date for Friday. Now, all I have to do is find a restaurant and call back the assistant to confirm the venue. I browse online to look for a restaurant when Drake knocks on the glass door. It makes that 'thunk, thunk' sound.

"Ready to leave?" Drake peers around the door as he holds it open.

"Of course." Fetching my purse in the drawer, I stand up and step past him.

There is something about this new Drake. It makes me feel uneasy. It's like my every move is being analyzed, he's studying me for some odd reason. Each time those steel, metal eyes zone in on me, I feel my heart palpitate. It's very disconcerting.

Mindy went to lunch five minutes ago, seemingly in a much better state than she was in earlier.

The elevator ride is, well, quiet. There's an uncomfortable silence, the easy feel kind, but crackling with tension, unsaid words and vehement intensity. I'm beginning to wonder if it's a wise idea to have agreed to have lunch with him.

In different circumstances, this would've been a given— doing a favor for a close family friend— working for him so he's taking that person to lunch, it would be considered normal, but things between us aren't normal and it's tiresome to pretend that it is.

The tension between us is incredibly palpable.

"My car is through here." Drake points at the entrance door. Of course, he won't be parking his car in the employee parking garage like the rest of us. His car is situated and parked conveniently up front.

"Swanky ride," I comment when he fishes out his keys and unlocks the doors to his silver Maserati.

"Thanks," Drake mumbles as he holds the door open and I swiftly slide onto the black leather seat. I pull the seatbelt and buckle myself in, cringing when I get a whiff of something feminine; a faint smell of perfume lingering on the black strappy belt. Is it Shannon's fragrance? Ugh!

When Drake finally rounds around the car, slides inside and starts the engine, my heart speeds up along with the speedometer. Good Lord, this man drives like he's racing in a Formula1.

"Will you calm it down a bit, Drake? I'd love to arrive at our destination in one piece."

"Anything for my Little One," he responds with endearment. Little One? He used to call me that and it would irk me like nothing else when we were younger, but once he told me why, I stopped getting upset about it. Drake felt I needed protection from all the bad things in life. Little One, weird much?

Drake quickly glances at me and for the very first time today, he smiles.

God, that smile . . . it used to make my stomach nosedive and silly little butterflies would flutter about. I may not be naïve and love-struck anymore, but it still does something to me. His killer smile accompanied with those gleaming, wicked eyes, it's a sight to behold. For a second—only for a second—I'm momentarily entranced.

My shrilling phone brings me out of my guileless, idiotic trance, though. I answer the call without glancing at the caller ID.

"Hello?"

"Miss Lily!" Jared drawls on the other end.

I smile at the sound of his voice. "Hey, hey!"

Jared chuckles. "What are your plans tonight? I want to take you out."

"Certainly, pick me up around six-thirtyish?" I happily reply to his question. Jared's a sweetheart. I'm really hoping this will turn into something good, something profound. So far, he's been passing with flying colors. Not only is he good with his oral skills, he makes the best pancakes.

Breakfast in bed is his thing and he spoils me rotten. After a quick goodbye, we end the call.

"Boyfriend?" Drake asks in a deadly tone. He's gripping the steering wheel a little tighter as he rubs it back and forth.

"He's getting there, yes."

"Hope said you don't have a boyfriend. When did this occur?" Drake asks in gritted tone.

"You talk to my mother about my love life?" I screech; a little bothered that he asks about me and my love life to my mother.

"Well, yeah. I do remember you exist, you know? Not like some other people I know," he shoots back.

You have got to be kidding me! We are not going there again. We keep going in circles and it's making me dizzy.

"Whatever. It doesn't matter." I shrug with pure indifference.

He grunts, but doesn't say much else for the rest of the car ride to the restaurant. I'm honestly fine with that, so it's a quiet until we arrive and are seated at his chosen destination.

6

8 Years Ago . . .

Playa del Carmen, México

Drake

I look at Lily's determined face. "OKAY—if this is what you want, then meet me on the veranda in fifteen minutes. Go get ready because there will be no backing out once you come to me. Think it through, okay?"

Lily merely smiles at me before she leaves. "No need, Drake. I'll be back in fifteen minutes."

I don't know exactly why I even offered, but what I do know is that I can't fathom another man touching her . . . let alone having Lily give up her innocence to some random guy. When she came up to me during New Year's Eve, blatantly offering that innocent body of hers, I wanted to succumb and devour her luscious lips on the spot; however, I stopped it before anything happened. You see, even if I found Lily sexy and beautiful, the minute my parents ever find out about us like that, wedding bells will start ringing in my ears and I sure as hell did not want that. Not at all.

I love women and I sure as hell am not ready to give up my freedom. I know my parents will expect me to marry Lily I am just not there with them on this one. Apart from her hot body and pretty face, it isn't enough for me to go in for the kill. Or kill myself in the process.

So, I steered clear away from her as much as I could until tonight. The thought of having her underneath me is already making me hard. She just expects me to pop her cherry, right? Nothing crazy afterwards . . . like an engagement ring? Fuck, I better make sure that she knows beforehand.

I stroll over to where the outdoor canopy is located. I stare at it and think, *I want to fuck her here. In the open and high from orgasms.* Yeah, I plan to take my sweet time with her, all night if I have to, because this will be the only time I am allowing myself to have her.

Fifteen minutes later, I have a hard time getting my thoughts in order. Lily Alexander struts out of the house with nothing on except a sheer, light pink baby doll nighty. My eyes instantly take in her breasts before traveling downwards to her bald mound. Fuck, she looks fucking incredible.

She looks at me nervously. "Drake?" she asks after a good minute of me not voicing a word out loud.

"Are you a hundred percent sure about this? Because once this happens . . . we can't undo it. I don't know if I can stop once we start." Fuck. I know that once I slip inside her, I'm not going to stop. The thought of taking her virginity is already too intoxicating.

Lily shakes her head. "No, I'm sure. I've been sure for a very long time." Her hazel eyes glitter as she looks at me with adoration and lust. I instantly get hard at the sultry look she gives me.

"Undress for me," I order. She immediately starts to unclasp the latch on the back of her baby doll and slowly takes it off her body; standing naked, proud and confident before me. I have a hard time taking my eyes off her beautiful body. "Go to the bed and spread your legs open."

Lily looks unsure as she bites her lips and stares at me for a few seconds. I raise my eyebrows, daring her to back out of her offer. I want her to be quite sure.

What comes from the pretty mouth almost undoes me. "Anything you want, Drake." She saunters past me and does as I asked her to.

Now it is my turn to be dumbstruck. Her pussy is untouched, perfect. My cock twitches and aches inside my pants, rigid with need.

My eyes gather in what is offered to me on that bed. I'm eager, and yet, hesitant, so I stand there, contemplating if I should carry on with what Lily has in mind.

"What are you waiting for, Drake? If you're about to change your mind, tell me, so I can leave. I'm done wasting my time on you."

Something inside me snaps to focus. I'm on the bed in a flash.

This woman is not going to get away. Hell to the motherfucking no, I think with blinded lust.

I kiss the sides of her lips and her jawline. "I've never had a virgin before, but I promise to make sure you will enjoy it as much as I will."

She writhes against my touch. Her body is fired up and ready to be conquered by me. "I don't care. I want you too much. So much, it hurts." She tells me as her fingers grab my shoulders.

Fuck, I want to bury my cock inside her so bad, but I have to slow down or I'll end up hurting her. I lower myself slowly onto her chest, letting the tip of my tongue flick her nipple and it hardens instantly. I lightly blow air against it and she begins to writhe more underneath me. Opening her legs wider, my cock perfectly sits against her pussy. Fuck, I tense up immediately when she started to grind it against her naked mound.

"Quit it, or I might end up taking you hard," I roughly pant out against her pebbled, rosebud nipple.

After a few seconds, I'm ready to move forward. My hands capture her supple breasts and tease them as my head and lips gradually move down towards her navel. My hot tongue sticks out and I let the wet tip move in achingly slow, agonizing, rhythmic circles around it.

"Oh, hell, Drake!" she moans, slowly rocking her body. "I want more. Give me more."

I want to laugh, but the deep ache in my groin knows the pain that she's going through. When my lips find her bald pussy, I delicately bite it. I can feel the heat of her sex on my face. I'm going to take my sweet time getting to know this fresh, virgin flesh before I annihilate it.

My lips seek the sides of her folds and gently suck on them, one after the other. My tongue leisurely snakes its way down the tiny area where her pussy and ass meets. "Touch me, please," my virgin temptress pleads.

Not yet, I think wickedly. I want her gushing out with wetness before I break her open. I want her to hunger for me; for my touch and my kiss before I flip her world upside down.

I want this night to be special.

So special, she will never forget it.

Never forget me.

Lily is thrashing when my mouth starts upwards again. I deliberately run my tongue along her wet core, past her hot entrance. My lips capture her nub and I lightly suck on it before my tongue swirls about, teasing her relentlessly. Lily's palms find the back of my head and urges me to do more. While my tongue is rooted on her nub, my right forefinger slowly makes its way in her wet and narrow channel. I take my time, making sure she savors each heightened stoke of my touch.

Her breathing is labored, panting as she begs me to end her agony. "Not yet, Little One. Once I know you are mindless with need, then I will take you, but until then, relish in the pleasure I give you. Revel in my touch and savor the journey."

My finger dips slowly inside her in acute circles. Her hot tunnel suctions it in, wanting it to go deeper into her moist depths. I'm so turned on, I feel my pre-cum slowly make its way out of the head of my shaft. I only use one finger and her pussy is already tight. How am I going to stretch her without causing much pain? It seems inevitable.

When my finger strokes deeper, her barrier stops me from going in further. Her insides are slick with wetness and I'm more than ready to possess this innocent body. I need to—have wanted to—for quite some time now. Lily has always been mine and it's time we both seal that ownership. To mark her—brand her—as mine, forever.

My mouth and fingers pull out from their ministrations. Hurriedly, I get rid of my clothes. I crawl up to her, seeking her lips as I gently, precisely nestle my rigid cock in between her wet, parted folds. We moan in unison when our lips touch.

"Taste yourself on my tongue, Babe." She slowly sucks on my tongue as she lavishes her pussy on me, gliding it back and forth against my hard cock.

"Take me, Drake. It's yours. Take it." I respond with kissing her, devouring her lips while I take hold of my cock and tease the entrance of her womanhood. "Make me yours," She begs in between my kisses.

Yes, she is mine.

My cock gently pierces her, but her pussy pushes it back out, certainly not used to it. My cock rejoices at this idea and I'm determined to claim it. I push the head back in with enough force to nudge past her wet, constricted passage. She loudly gasps as she feels the head of my shaft invade her virgin channel. I stop kissing her then, since my breathing and heart rate accelerate rapidly. All the blood in me goes south and pounds in my cock as it plunges deeper. We both halt our breathing when it hits her thin barrier.

"Are you ready for me?" I manage to croak out. My cock pulsates inside her.

"For you, always," Lily breathes out as our eyes clash.

I know deep down she means every word. I also know that she's in love with me and at this very moment, time stands still as I gaze down on the woman who just captured my heart. I have always loved her, but now, I realize, I really am so deeply in love with her that it scares the crap out of me. When I feel her shift sideways, my cock instantly twitches. Not willing to dwell on my thoughts, I make love to her lips as I simultaneously pull my hips back, letting the tip of my shaft stay inside of her before I plunge into it again. This time, when I repeat the stroke, I grab both of her hips and ram it hard, breaking it, in one swift fluid thrust. I capture her lips and muffle her cries with my kisses as my cock slowly makes love to her.

Mine.

All mine.

When her body finally gets used to my invasion of hers, her muscles start to relax. Lily can barely control her moans of pleasure as she begs for more.

"I need to possess you," I groan wretchedly against her ear.

"Possess what's yours, Drake." Lily barely finishes whispering those words when I begin to pound her, relentlessly. The sexy sounds she makes urges me to take her harder. I feel her muscles contract around my shaft as she readies for her own release. Lily yelps out a sob when the orgasm blasts through her while I fuck her like I'm being chased. "I love you," she sobs repeatedly.

My body tenses as my cum builds up, ready to be freed. It takes a few more strokes before I shoot my semen inside her, screaming her name, recklessly.

After we are both starting to breathe normally, I roll off her and gather her in my arms. Lily immediately passes out.

Even though I just realized I love her the way she loves me, I'm not ready to give whatever it is she desires from me. The stakes are too high when it comes to Lily. Maybe in a year or two, but not right now, I know I'm not ready.

After an hour or so, I gather her satiated limp body and place her inside her room. I don't sleep a wink as I think of a way out. I make sure the maids are awake before I leave the villa and go back to New York.

I could easily reason with my parents if they ask about my sudden departure, but I simply can't reason if the woman I love, wakes up and asks me to stay. After the kind of earth-shattering night we've had, I'm convinced that Lily has the power to break me in two and I'm not ready to have someone rule me like that.

Not yet, anyway.

7

Present

Lily

We are in Santa Monica seated at a restaurant on Ocean Drive; it overlooks the beautiful Pacific. My mood and spirit lift at the sound of the waves and sea gulls that permeate the air.

The restaurant is a few minutes from my home, but I don't dare mention that to him. It isn't a big deal, yet, I just don't want to tell him that. I know it will only take a phone call to know my information, but still.

We just ordered and are both quiet as we look out at the view of the beach. The silence is uncomfortable, to say the least. I remember Drake and I used to be very close. We were until I threw myself at him during New Year's. To this day, I admit that I feel stupid for ruining my friendship with him. Yeah, he's a jackass now, but he wasn't before. Now, after eight long years of not seeing each other, there's so much to say, but there's nothing we want to voice.

The tension I feel coming off him is blatant.

Sighing, I cock a quick glance at him, catching my breath when I meet his eyes that are looking serious as hell. What the hell is he thinking now? I raise my brow in question to him, but he just keeps on staring, like I'm such a weird specimen.

"Darling, here you are!" A saccharine voice speaks behind me. I tense when I see Drake's facial expression change and become guarded.

"What are you doing here?" Drake utters through gritted teeth.

When the woman in question finally stops at our table, I see a beautiful blonde with hazel eyes that are framed with the longest lashes I have ever seen. I suppose this is Drake's girlfriend or fiancée... whatever the hell she is? I see her measure me up and down while smiling sweetly at me. That makes me not like her on the spot.

Fake. She's a fucking fake. I hate women like her.

I mean, what is the point in trying to be nice and all when you obviously don't like the person? She rounds Drake's side of the table and pulls herself a chair. Obviously, the faker wants to join us. How quaint. I simmer some more.

"Who told you I was here?" Drake eyes her with a hard stare when Shannon tries to get comfortable on her chair. Her stupid fake smile still plastered on her pretty face.

"I called the office, of course. Mindy gave me the information, albeit reluctantly." Shannon pouts at Drake. Does her stupid fake smile and those stupid pouts always work? How cheesy is that of Drake? Triple ick.

"Did you need something? You could've called at least." Drake's tone is obviously hard and he's not pleased, but that doesn't seem to faze Shannon. Guess he's not so easily won over, after all.

She looks at me then, still smiling, and speaks, "I know, Darling, but I wanted to meet your new assistant. When Mindy informed me that you took her out, I was . . . curious."

Drake clears his throat and introduces us. I'm a little miffed that he doesn't even mention that I'm a family friend or that we grew up together. "Do you not notice that I'm in a middle of a work day, Shannon? Couldn't it have waited?"

Shannon places her coral lacquered nails on Drake's shoulder and strokes it sensually. She purrs next to his ears. "Darling, Daddy wants you to call him. It's about the wedding and the date. He was hoping you could fill the bill for everything. Now, go scoot and make that call, please?"

Drake curses and gets up to make a call to Shannon's father. When Drake is nowhere in sight, the real woman comes out.

"If you're thinking about bagging your boss, I will fucking mess with your life. Drake's mine, so don't make the same mistake the woman before you did. I can get you fired in a blink of an eye. Drake loves me and he'll do anything to please me. I will keep an eye on you, Lily."

Shannon is dead serious, too. I want to laugh so hard, and yet, throw the entire glass of water at this yapping woman.

How in the world did Drake manage to be with this woman? Now I get what Patricia was talking about. Shannon is simply mental and off her rocker.

"I'm not interested in Drake. You can have him for yourself for all I care, but you, Shannon, need to watch your tongue because when I fucking hit back, I fucking hit you back hard. I'm not one for cat fights, but I can take you on. You threaten me and then expect me to just clamor up? You've picked the wrong woman to threaten and intimidate. I don't give a rat's ass about you, a wannabe actress, who wants to nab a rich guy. I don't care, got that, blondie?"

Shannon's eyes become so dark they're almost black. Her neck is turning red and I can see it is starting to creep up all the way to her cheeks. If she is going to have a heart attack right now, I will probably just sit back and watch her drop on the floor without a tinge of a muscle to help. Wretched bitches don't deserve pity. I can be a cold-hearted bitch if I want to. Sadly, it was Drake who taught me to be one.

She is almost tomato red. I can see she wants to kill me, but Drake chooses that moment to rejoin our party. His eyes swing back and forth, noticing his fiancée's beet red-colored state. My eyes never leave Shannon. What comes out of her mouth isn't a surprise. "You're fired, Lily. You can kiss your job goodbye and go back to wherever shady part of town you came from. No one gets to talk to me so disrespectfully and get away with it."

I bite my lip as I look at her with amusement, trying to hold back my laughter.

Drake interjects, "What the fuck's going on here? You can't fire her—"

"Of course, I can. We'll be married soon and the company's going to be part mine." Shannon directs her gaze at me. "What are you still doing here, looking amused? You can leave now. You're not needed."

That does it.

I roar in laughing hysterics. I start to cry tears of joy when I hear Drake join in. Goodness this woman takes delusional to another level. To think that Hugh would hand her a partial part of the company is unrealistic. The man worked hard to get where he's at in his life. He's not going to risk being a pauper by giving some of those riches off to some gold-digger.

The horror on Shannon's face is beyond ridiculous.

After a good few minutes of barking my amusement, I use the linen napkin to wipe my tear-stained face. "I can't fire Lily simply because mother hired her. Second, if I do choose to fire her, my parents will disown me in a heartbeat. Third, Lily doesn't live in a shady part of anywhere. She inherited half of her father's worth when he died." Drake clears his throat and looks at Shannon. "I think you better leave. You can move out of my home while you're at it. Leave the keys on the kitchen counter. Bye, Shannon."

She stands instantly up in rage and slaps Drake on his cheek, leaving a red spot. "You, son of a bitch! You're not going to get away with this." Shannon threatens before she scampers out of the restaurant in furious haste.

I gasp and stare at Drake while he rubs his cheek. "So, that was Shannon, huh?"

Drake's eyes twinkle. "You find this funny, don't you? Just as well. That woman was becoming a nightmare."

Interesting. Wasn't he planning to marry her? "Um, so I guess there's no wedding then?"

Drake sighs and looks away. His eyes seem distant as he watches the beach. He looks sad. If Shannon meant so much to him... then why break up with her?

"I never wanted to get married . . . well not right away, and especially, not with her," Drake says, breaking the silence.

He waits until the waiter is done placing our food on the table before starting again. "Four months ago, Shannon was pregnant. I know it's not enough reason to marry someone, but I want to offer my child the same childhood I had, with two loving parents. My parents didn't know that she was pregnant. I was going to tell them, eventually, but there was never a right time, you know? Shannon miscarried during her sixteenth week. I was going to tell her that the wedding was not going to happen, but each time I tried, she would go into a crazy meltdown. She almost killed herself once. After that incident, I was complacent and told myself that I will wait for a few more months before I break it off with her. I wanted her to seek professional help, but she insisted that she was fine. Anyway, that's the story behind Shannon and me." Drake takes a lengthy sip of his water and starts to eat his meal.

I stare at him in astonishment. How could he just eat after the shocking information he just bombarded me with? "What if she tries to kill herself again, what are you going to do?"

"That's her family's problem now. Her parents know how their daughter is, but they just brush it off. If they can do that, so can I. Shannon used her pregnancy and miscarriage for far too long. I am well over it."

"I'm sorry about the baby," I murmur.

He shrugs. "Yeah, but it was for the best. I don't honestly think she and I would've been any good as parents anyway. I can always be grateful for that, I suppose."

I'm still reeling from all the insane information. I can barely even manage to put the food in my mouth, let alone swallow it. Drake, a father... it's the most bizarre thought. He's never been keen on kids. I mean he finds them cute, but he stays away from them like they were diseased or something. I guess that was the old Drake. The new one might actually love to have babies. I suppose I really don't know this man anymore.

After that eventful lunch, Drake hands me a spare key for his house and gives me some other important details that are essential for me to know, like where he gets his dry cleaning done and so forth.

=====

When the clock hits five pm, I get up and gather my belongings. I glance towards the door when I hear a knock.

It's Drake.

"There's an event tomorrow night. I will send a car at six to get you."

Um, you mention this now? "Do I have to be there? I don't think I'll be necessary." I don't want to be an idiot accessory, either.

"It's work related. You will meet a lot of our contacts and it's good for you to know who they are." Sigh. Of course he brings up work.

Shit.

I nod. "Okay, six tomorrow night." I get up, sort out my things, and shove whatever it is that I need in my tote purse. When I hear him clear his throat, I'm a little startled. He didn't leave yet? I thought he left already.

"Yes?" I ask, not glancing in his direction.

"I won't be here tomorrow, so I will see you at the event. Mindy will have all the information on your desk tomorrow morning. She already picked up the dry cleaning, so you don't have to do it any longer."

Thank God for Mindy. I totally forgot about his other demands. He also added that Skull was already taken care of. Okay.

"So, I guess I will see you tomorrow night?" He lingers longer.

Does he plan to leave any second now?

"Yes, Drake, I will be there tomorrow night." I gather up my things and stride towards the door. I frustratingly halt when he blocks my passage.

I groan. "What now?"

"Do you need a ride home?" he whispers sultrily at me. His eyes focus on my lips.

I need to get out of here, NOW! "I drove here. I have to go. I have things to do. Will you move out of my way, Drake?" I try not to look at him directly. I simply can't. I don't have it in me to do so.

"You have plans tonight? A date with that boyfriend of yours, perhaps?"

"What is this, twenty questions? You already know that I do. Drop it, will you? You're starting to get on my nerves!" I exclaim with passion, but the man is being infuriatingly dense.

"I was just curious, Lil. I haven't seen you in almost a decade. I suppose you can say that I miss making you blush. You're blushing now and I must say I like this look better on you." A devilish grin suddenly emerges as he eyes me closer as if in inspection, again.

Not today, Drake, or ever AGAIN will I succumb to you. Once was lesson enough.

Without blinking, I speak with utmost certainty. "I am not interested, Drake. So, please, do us both a favor and drop the Mr. Seduction act because it will never work on me."

Drake moves closer, our chests touching. I instantly try to pull away, but he has my shoulders on lockdown. "Why do you tense up when I'm close to you, Lil?" Drake painstakingly brushes my cheek and I look away and try to avoid his touch. "Or why does your breathing become shallow…" Drake whispers as he draws himself closer. All air leaves me when I feel his hot breath against my ear. "You still want me, but you're fighting it."

Fine, maybe I still do, but that doesn't mean I'll act on it.

"Dream on, Drake." I forcefully push him aside and stride out of my office. It doesn't take him long to catch up with me as I wait for the elevator.

The man is beyond exasperating! He makes me want to commit bloody murder.

I don't acknowledge him when he jumps next to me inside the elevator.

"Do you want to go out for dinner?" Drake annoyingly asks.

For the love of God! Leave me alone! I want to scream, yet, I hold myself in check. I can't lose my temper on my first day of work. Although, I'm tempted... oh, so tempted.

"Nope, I'm going out with Jared. Remember?" I almost feel triumphant when I don't hear a smart comeback. It only lasts briefly.

"Is Jared staying over at your place, too?" he finally speaks, his voice low, but succinct.

I glare at him. With both of my hands on my hips, I tell him off. "My sex life is none of your business. Who I fuck and don't fuck is irrelevant. This interrogation ends now."

"For now," Drake states in a matter-of-fact tone, but I completely ignore him.

I don't even bother to respond because the elevator doors open. I hurriedly scramble out and into the lobby and race towards the parking structure.

Once I'm in traffic, I begin to fume some more. "Fuck you, Drake Tatum." I swear. Drake is royally screwing with my head and I hate it.

8

The fundraiser event for independent films is held at The Beverly Hills Hotel in The Crystal Ballroom. It's illuminated with subtle pinkish-lavender lighting and each table is decorated with white orchids. The ambiance is dreamy and the soft jazz eases some of my tension.

I'm sipping my champagne when I feel a zinging sensation on the back of my neck all the way down my spine. There is only one man who can make me feel like a fucking magnet and that is Drake. Knowing he's close by, I don't even bother to look for him. Instead, I opt to savor the beautiful surroundings and the beautiful ambiance.

"Lily."

Guess that didn't last long. I spin around and greet him, bitingly, "Drake." I briefly assess him, looking handsomely dapper as ever, but I force my eyes to drag away from his striking features. *I am not going to dwell about this man,* I repeat many times in my head.

"You look gorgeous. Gold suits you. It brings out your eyes," he compliments as his eyes gingerly rove over my body. Admiration clearly stated in those metallic orbs.

Well, heck, I didn't plan to look like crap even though it crossed my mind, once. Or twice. Instead, I wore a tight-fitted, body-hugging, gold sheath dress that exposes my entire back with a slit up one leg. My hair is stylishly piled on top of the crown of my head.

"Did you need something?" I go back to my old pose, trying to block out his handsome face.

He comes closer. Drake stands behind me, brushing my butt softly against his thigh. "You can't expect to ask me that question and not get hard. I always need you, it seems." His lips caress the tip of my ear.

I simply shudder and try to ignore the tell-tale signs of my own arousal. "Stop being a twit and start thinking with your head, Drake. And I mean the head up there and not down south, nestled in between your legs." I bring the point home by poking my finger at his topmost head.

Drake roars with amused laughter. "That sharp wit of yours, Babe, it will get you in trouble. I get turned on more when you whiplash me with your words. I can't help it. You're sexy as hell . . . and that dress is giving me all sorts of ideas . . ." Drake uses the back of his fingers to trace my naked back and doesn't stop until it reaches the top of my ass. "I do so want to rip this off your body. You naked with your heels on and nothing else . . . bent over and ready to be mounted."

Mother of God! What in the world?! "Damn it, Drake. We're at a fucking event. Stop being such a horny kid and focus," I chide him, but to no avail.

"You can't dress like this, dangle this sinful body of yours, and not expect me to react." Drake moves closer, his state of arousal hard against my butt cheek. I try to compose myself before I pass out from the feel of it. "Behave yourself tonight. I don't want you talking to other men."

I straighten up, tense. "You wish."

"Don't push it, Lily. You've been running away from me for too long. That's coming to a close. I will possess every inch of you, soon… very soon." Drake's deadly warning pins me on the spot, but I will not be threatened.

"Not yours, Drake. Now, go find your seat and be a good boy. I will find mine. I'll see you around."

When Mindy made the reservations, she had assumed that Shannon was going to be with Drake tonight, so our seating arrangements are different. I am grateful for it since the tension is too much with him. I can only take it in small doses.

Of course, Drake sits with The VIP's while I sit next to the minions, but I don't mind it. In fact, I have a blast. Chris, a guy who works at one of the most sought after PR firms in Hollywood, is quite entertaining. His stories about celebrities are hilarious. It actually drowns out whoever is talking and making a speech about so and so. Yeah, I don't pay much attention on those since Chris's storytelling is much livelier and not as much of a snooze fest by some stuck-up CEO.

I'm already on my fourth champagne flute by the time dessert rolls in when Chris asks me to dance, I delightfully say yes. He chooses a spot where it is dark and secluded. I don't mind since he is quite attractive with his brown hair, mini-faux hawk and chocolate brown eyes. Chris holds me close against him as we dance to the slow jazz beat.

We're not dancing for long before a gruff voice comes out from behind me. "Excuse me, but I need my assistant. Right *now*," Drake barks while Chris apologizes as he recognizes who Drake is.

When Chris leaves, Drake orders me to follow him outside. His chilly demeanor makes me nervous. Drake leads me to the garden, away from the fountains and the noise, behind some tall bushes. Once we are out of earshot, all hell breaks loose.

"How dare you defy my order! Did you enjoy flaunting him to me?" It's dark, and yet, I can still see the anger profoundly etched across his face.

"I wasn't thinking... honestly, I forgot about you for a bit."

That stops him. "Did you just tell me that . . . you forgot about me?"

I lick my lips nervously as I look away. "Well, newsflash, Buddy. You're not the only attractive man living on the planet."

Drake cusses me out before he moves in and before I know it, he is biting my lips hard and devouring them. I don't even hesitate to respond when he growls as one of his hands seeks the slit of my dress and roughly pushes my underwear aside. I mindlessly writhe against him as he drives his middle finger inside me while his thumb crushes my clit. In a minute, I'm coming apart from his fingers.

"What you said is true . . . but there is only one man that is meant for you . . . and you are staring at him, moaning his name as you come beautifully on his fingers. Stop fighting it, because I have. I'm yours."

======

What the hell just happened? "Will you please take your fingers off me?" I'm red with shame and totally beyond humiliated.

Drake takes his fingers off, but fixes my underwear back beforehand. He leans over and kisses the tip of my nose. "I guess you're still rejecting the idea of us?"

"Damn right, I am. I want to go home now, Drake. I am done playing your games."

Drake is silent while he stands there watching me. "You're tired and clearly drunk. You need to rest before we leave for Greece on Sunday."

"Greece?" I croak. He never mentioned anything about Greece. Well, his agenda has been curiously absent of a few things. Drake seems to love throwing events at me quite unexpectedly.

"One of the biggest investments we have made this year. The movie is called Blasphemous with Bass Cole. I have to see how everything is going and check if they need more for the budget or what not."

"How long will we be there?" My heart hammers against my chest. I know what this is. Drake is going in for the kill. He is going to drive me crazy until I give it up to him. I haven't forgotten his ever reliable tactic for women; he's used it ever since we were kids.

"More or less, three days."

That's hell of a long time. A day is enough to drive me mental with him. Three days is surely going to put me on suicide watch. "Work . . . I will work . . . but the underlying agenda you have, Drake, won't happen."

"We shall soon find out, Little One."

Precise. Cold. And fucking determined.

9

Drake, as promised, picks me up at three in the afternoon in a hired limo. Not saying much to each other, he takes my luggage and hands it the driver. I mumble my thanks to the cheery looking chauffer.

Why is Drake in a bad mood anyway? Am I not the one he humiliated at the event? Aren't I the one who got the tongue attack from his crazy ex-fiancée? I know he's finished with her, but I'm still a little baffled as to why a man like Drake would want to date a woman like Shannon Mallory in the first place. Sure, she's pretty to look at, but surely there's more to a relationship than just wild sex? Well, if the man in question is Drake, I'm sure IQ isn't necessary. He just loves his women to be good to look at from what I noticed and heard.

I suppose that says a lot about him, doesn't it? How disappointing.

Since we're travelling, I have donned a pair of comfortable black leggings and a black shirt with my Tory Burch flats. I loaded up my E-reader earlier to make sure that I'll have all the books that I need to catch up on ready and waiting, but I'm not too sure if I will have enough time to read once we get there, since we're going to check out the Blasphemous film-shooting. I am super excited to see and meet the men of the movie. I am a mega fan when it comes to Bass Cole. Though I don't mention this to Drake, he might think that I'm unprofessional if he finds out that I am a diehard fan of one of the actors in the film that they're backing.

We are in the first-class cabin and somewhere above the Atlantic Ocean when he finally starts a conversation with me. "What happened with that first boyfriend of yours, Aaron, was it?"

I gasp. What the fuck!?

Drake sees my shocked expression and offers an explanation. "Your mom . . . She told me after I kept nagging her for a while."

I put down my e-reader and eye him cautiously. "Why are you so interested about my past?"

Drake nonchalantly shakes his head before he responds, "I wanted to know if you had moved on. I was curious, I guess."

Right, of course, since I blurted it out that I loved him that night in Mexico; he had probably wanted to make sure that I wasn't in love with him anymore.

"Aaron was great. You know first love and what not. We were together for two years and decided it wasn't working out anymore. So, we amicably parted ways. I still talk to him from time to time." I pick up my e-reader again and continue to read my book. After a few minutes, he speaks up again.

"Funny, I thought I was your first love." Drake toys with his whiskey before he takes a sip.

"Huh? That is funny." Fuck, don't embarrass me, Drake! Drop the fucking subject already. Let it slide, please.

"Why did you tell me I was, then?" Drake picks up his whiskey, drains it and places the cup back on the tray, his eyes stay glued on the glass before him.

"I don't want to go back there, Drake." I meant it, too. That night is best forgotten. I can't bring it up with him. Especially, since I have no means to escape the conversation in the damn airplane . . . then it occurs to me that maybe this was his plan after all . . .

Clear gray eyes clash with mine. Somehow, there is sadness in them. "What if I want to go back there and dig it up? We have to talk about it, Lil."

I know, but not right now, we aren't. "Later, when I am ready to do so, let's leave it at that for now."

"As you wish, Little One."

=====

"Lil?" Drake asks next to me.

The entire cabin is quiet and everyone is fast asleep. I was about to join in their peaceful slumber, but the annoying man next to me keeps me up.

"Yes, Drake?" I ask, exasperated.

"When you think of being married to someone, who comes to your mind?"

Is he fishing for some information? That will never happen. As if I will dish out to him.

"No one, really. Marriage is not something I dwell on." Well, not anymore, I don't.

"My parents think I shouldn't marry anyone that isn't you. Do you think they're right?" Drake keeps pressing the stupid subject.

Kill me now, please. "Your parents always wanted that, but they're wrong. We both know that."

"I thought they were. Now, it looks like they were right all along."

That makes me look at him. "Can you shut the hell up already? This is getting icky, Drake. We were through before we even began. There's no going around it, no matter how we rehash things. You left me. You asked me to move on. And I did. I did as you asked me to. Now, you want to press rewind? I'm afraid I can't do that. Not even for you."

"If you want me to give up, it won't happen. Even if you wish it hard enough to happen, Lil, because I haven't been this sure of anything in my life—and I want you in it. In you, with you, day in and day out. That's all I know and if you ask me to see reason, I am seeing it. You are my reason. It took me eight years to see it, but now that I have. I am taking action." He halts and makes sure I stare at him, understanding him with full certainty, before he speaks again. "Run if you must, Lily. I will catch you, either way. Do not doubt that."

I will resist you. I won't give in until I have no strength in me left.

10

The island of Aspasia is a jewel. It's even more beautiful than I could ever imagine.

"Wow." I admire the view on the patio that gives access to the beach.

"Yeah, it is gorgeous out here. Listen, Bass and Emma are still shooting. This is their cottage and there are two more spare rooms. You can go and take your pick."

Something dislodges in my throat. I'm sharing a roof with Bass Cole? Mother of God! I think I have gone straight to Heaven! "Bass Cole . . . in the same house . . . I think I need to sit down for that." I start to fan myself with my right hand, while my excitement runs riot in my head.

"Isn't he a little too young for you?" Drake leans against the stone railing while he watched me getting all hyped up.

"Who cares about age when a guy looks like Bass? He's like... the most beautiful man . . ." I murmur as I picture the actor in that vampire movie of his and what a movie that was. Sex God, your name is Bass Cole!

Drake walks towards where I am sitting and yanks me off the chair. "Hey! What the hell is your problem?" I yelp and slap his hand that is clutching my arm, but to no avail.

He drags me all the way inside and pushes me against a wall. My breathing is frantic when I see the stormy eyes that meet me. "You better not fuck anyone here, Lil. There will be hell to pay if you do. I don't want you talking to any man for that matter."

My hand instantly slaps him. He has gall to manhandle me and issue orders. "If you think for a second that I will let you run around and dictate me, well tough, I am not that woman. I have my own mind, my own wants and my own needs. How I come about in achieving them is my business. Best you get that in that semi-insipid brain of yours because you missed the memo, Drake. I am not yours. Never was." I press my hands on his torso and try to push him off me, but he's way too heavy and way too pumped up to be moved.

Our noses are touching, our lips only a hairsbreadth away from brushing. I dare not snake my tongue out to lick my lips because this infuriating man might just take that as his cue to claim me for a kiss.

"I did get the memo, Lil. My fate was sealed the moment you were born into this world. You were mine since day one. You were definitely mine when I took your virginity. Do you honestly think that I would let you give your virginity away to any man? No, over my dead body, and you know it, too. You were mine then, and you are mine now."

"This body hasn't been yours for the last eight years, Drake."

I close my eyes when he presses his body against mine. The stone wall is cold against my back and I shiver when I feel his breath on my neck. The tip of his nose brushes against my jaw, smelling me like I'm his meal, his woman, his property; but I am no longer his. Best he realizes that.

"How many?" Drake whispers against my ear. I flinch when the wet, hot tip of his tongue tastes my earlobe.

"How many, what?"

"Men . . . I want numbers, Lily." Drake suddenly sounds menacing.

But . . . why? Sure, he maybe lusting for me now, but it sure was not the case eight years ago. Again, why now?

"I am not going to answer that. Let me go, Drake. Jared and I... I'm ready to be with him." I have been thinking about it. A lot. Jared is a decent and sweet guy. To top that off, he is funny and easy to be around. Jared told me two nights ago that he wants things to be serious between us. I have yet to give him a proper answer, but it will be a definite yes.

"No, you're not. How can you be ready, Lil? You can barely hide the fact that you want me. I still affect you . . . I know this because you still look like you're in love with me."

I feel like he just slapped me. My hand lifts again, ready to slap some sense into him, but he catches it this time. The steel band of his hand on my wrist is unyielding. "I love this temper of yours. It's going to be fun unleashing this temperamental side of you while I dominate you in bed." His hips push against me and his hard arousal makes me shudder. "Now that we're back in each other's lives, there will be no other man for you, except me. I don't want anyone, but you. It's time we submit to it... to what is meant for us. I am ready for you now, Lil."

Huh? He's ready? How laughable because I sure as hell am not.

"I don't feel the same. I don't want you like that... Physically, yes, you're very attractive, but emotionally, you're not for me. Never were, so let's drop it. This woman is not interested in your sexual prowess. Get off me before I knee your blessed balls."

His nose flares while his eyes rage. "You will come to me. I am sure of it. Once you do, don't expect me to let you go again because I won't and don't ever plan to. I'm counting down the hours until you come to me." Drake speaks in a clipped tone before he finally releases my tense body.

After another hard stare, he spins around and goes to his room, striding ever so confidently. While I stand here, taken aback... troubled and dumbfounded more than ever.

What gets to me most are his parting words. The way he said them, it was like he knows. Does he think that since he's ready for me that I'll just happily oblige and let him back in?

He can think again.

=====

Both Bass Cole and Emma Anderson come back to the villa a couple of hours later, just before six in the evening. I'm really unprepared when I come face-to-face with the very masculine, blonde, blue-eyed star.

"This is my assistant and childhood best friend, Lily."

Drake introduces us all. Emma is sweet and strikingly pretty. To me, she looks like a goddess, but what catches my attention is Bass himself.

"How are you finding the island so far? It's gorgeous around here, isn't it?" Bass smiles at me. Like a stupid puppy, I'm just in awe of him.

Drake nudges me. "I'm sorry. I'm just a big fan. I love your movies!" I gush at the smiling Bass.

"Thank you, Lily. Do you mind telling this woman how great I am? She's being a brat." Bass takes hold of Emma and kisses her forehead.

It's obvious how crazy he is about her. Watching them laugh before they excuse themselves to get ready before dinner is nice to see.

"You totally looked stupid just then, Lil." Drake is being a dick again.

"Whatever, you just wish you looked like that. Damn, those two look great together." I smile before I go out to the patio and stroll towards the beach.

I'm just in time to watch the sunset. It's glorious. The slight breeze is crisp, just enough to cool the skin. I take off my sandals and stand barefoot on the shore. The tide brushing against my feet is relaxing.

The day after tomorrow, I will be back in LA. Back to my home and away from Drake. I don't mind working for him, but being around him all day and night is definitely driving me nuts. He's insufferable, stubborn and he makes me want to gouge his eyes out. There are times, though . . . I just want to kiss him senseless.

"I can't help that I'm a jealous bastard. I don't like it when you smile at another guy like that. I know you didn't mean anything by it, but shit—I still don't like it," Drake speaks from behind me.

Oh come on, it's Bass Cole. It was a given for anyone with eyes.

"Yeah, well, it's bullshit. You have no grounds to be jealous, Drake. Get that through your head. Acting like a jealous, possessive lover is dumb when you mean nothing to me."

Drake stands behind me, lips against my ear, cutting through my delicate armor.

"Ouch, that tongue of yours really needs some kind of punishment. I am possessive of what's mine. You were mine the moment you surrendered this body to me eight years ago. I'm back and I don't want to relinquish that right. However long it takes, I will fucking have you back. I won't have it any other way. Get that through your head, Lily." He abruptly leaves afterward his speech.

I still stand there like a frozen statue, his words playing around in my head. He might be right, but I will not submit that easily, not without kicking and screaming with protest.

"Are you okay?" Emma asks as she comes up next to me. Her beautiful, big, blue eyes look concerned.

"Yes. Drake's just being . . . a dick. Nothing new there, if you ask me." I smile when she starts laughing.

"Yeah, I could tell he was getting all territorial. Men can't help it. They act like idiots when they really like someone." Emma stares out at the horizon, looking like her thoughts brought her somewhere far away.

"You and Bass look perfect. He's crazy about you," I say, changing the subject. I know I'm getting personal, but Emma has that easy personality that I feel comfortable talking to, like normal friends do.

Emma shakes her head, but her eyes speak volumes. "I think he does . . . he's been terrific. No, no, he's been perfect . . . Amazing to the point where . . . I feel that we should slow down." She quickly glances at me before continuing. "Sorry for dumping that on you, I just miss having my friends around. I don't have an emotional outlet about men right now. They'll be here in a few days, though, and I'm excited about that."

"Trust me. Your problem is much better than mine. I'd rather listen to yours than go through mine in my head for the thousandth time. I was in love with him eight years ago. After spending a night in his arms, my first, he left without a word and now he just expects me to fall back into his arms again."

"Maybe a good talk would do the trick for you both. From what I could see earlier, he's got it bad for you and I don't think Drake's the kind of man to back down, anyway. Just follow your heart, that's what I used to tell myself." Emma looks thoughtful a moment.

"You guys are in love, huh?"

Emma looks at me strangely, shaking her head and huffing. "No, no, we just started barely a week ago. It's too early. I just got off a relationship a few months back." Emma bites her lip nervously. "It's just too early . . . It just can't happen . . ." she wonders out loud.

I touch her shoulder and squeeze it. "Trust me, Hon, love is a bitch. It creeps up on you when you don't want it to."

Emma sighs. "Shit. I don't want to think about any of it. Let's go get some dinner and get drunk. I think we both need it."

That's more like it.

That I can agree on. "Awesome, lead the way."

=====

The next day, Emma has to shoot scenes with her co-stars, and Bass has to go to New York for some work involving the third installment of Knights of the Cimmerian that is going to be out in a few months.

I was at the meeting Drake held earlier with Martin Lombardo, the director, and some other important people involving the movie. The meeting took almost two hours and when it ended, I was ready to hit the sack. The time difference really is too difficult to adjust to when I've only been here for a couple of days. It's a bitch, but I know I have to deal with it.

Drake is supposed to be meeting up with a few people. I'm relieved since I don't really want to do anything unless it involves passing out for the rest of the night.

Which I do, gladly.

When I wake the next day, it's already time to leave for London.

11

The last couple of days with Drake are challenging and strenuous and I am exhausted physically, mentally and emotionally.

I am teetering on the edge of the precipice and I'm a step away from surrendering to what he wants . . . to what my body's been longing and yearning for.

It's been over five hours since we departed from Heathrow. Six long, arduous and crucial hours... ticking slowly by until we land in Los Angeles.

Good luck to me.

I shift again, a little uncomfortable. The silent humming noise of the aircraft's engine lulls people to sleep as we cross the Atlantic Ocean. The past few days flash in my head.

Spending three whole, damn days with Drake took a toll on me.

I am confused as ever, maybe more so.

One side is telling me to never forget about the past and the other one tells me to hell with it, just surrender to him. I admit the second choice is seriously starting to appeal to me as the minutes tick by.

Could I separate having sex and my emotional being?

Could I be that mechanical? I know a lot of people do it. Heck, my friends do it all the time, but I never have . . . What Drake did to me ages ago made me hesitant. I only get involved sexually with men that I have been dating seriously.

Curled in my seat, I stare at the back of the woman who is across the aisle from me, snoring lightly, while my thoughts run amok.

"Are you awake, Babe?" Drake gently asks behind me. He is so close I can feel his hot breath on the back of my neck.

My body tenses as each of his labored breaths hit my skin. I bite my lip hard, trying not to groan and moan at the same time. Drake is definitely making things difficult now. When I'm certain that I can't take any more of the toe-curling torture, I shift onto my other side and face him.

"What do you want?" I ask in a gritted, hushed tone.

The dim lighting of the cabin makes his eyes glow. Desire and lust are tangible in those silver orbs. Instead of responding to my question, Drake nudges his head closer against the laid back seat and stares some more. His eyes take me in, stroking as he studies my profile. Starting from the base of my throat, his gaze slowly and heatedly caresses me; it makes me tremble as it drifts higher.

Drake hasn't even touched me and I'm ready to come apart. His power over my body is beyond ridiculous, and yet, it's something I crave. It is something I haven't experienced with anyone else, except Drake, and now that I've been reminded of it, its compelling power is hypnotizing and simply binds me towards him like a fucking magnet.

His face is so close our eyes clash. Drake's eyes challenge me. He obviously wants me to make the first move. Have I made my decision? Am I sure enough that I can withstand this once it's done between him and I?

Oh, just fuck it! "I want you," I murmur before I bite his bottom lip. I hear him groan before he pulls my head towards him, a little too hard, but I like it.

I know Drake is a passionate man with insatiable appetites, but the way he is ravening my lips with a wolfish hunger, I'm beginning to think that I was his last meal.

With our lips on a wet-hungered lip lock, my hands reacquaint themselves with his body. The dull ache and the ambush of nostalgia come in spades.

I'm eighteen again. In his arms, he makes me feel like the Lily I once was. In love and worshipping the ground this man walks on. The overwhelming tidal wave of old emotions burns something inside me. The more Drake and I kiss, the burning becomes much more intense. It's addictive. Like getting high the first time and I want more of my drug.

I lift his shirt and run my nails from his chest all the way to his abs. Drake's grip on the back of my head tightens. My hand goes lower and rubs his palpable hard-on. The more I rub and stroke it, the bigger it becomes.

Sex starved? Yes, that would be me.

I am heady with erotically aroused senses and my hand seems to have its own mind because it won't part with his crotch. Drake breaks the kiss and rests his head against the headrest. "Lil, you're killing me here. Unless . . . if you don't have any plans to stop."

I sensually bite my lip while my heart speeds frantically against my chest as I look at Drake's sexually charged profile. "Do you want to . . . fuck me here?" I whisper excitedly.

Drake's large hand goes over my hand that is still rubbing him. His hand tightens against mine as he leans over and brushes his lips against mine. "I want to fuck you anywhere I can get you. You should know that by now. I want to feel those wet folds glide against my cock while I fuck your pussy well. I want you. I have always wanted you, always."

Shit. That admission soaks my panties. "Claim me, Drake." Again.

"Turn around and lift your hips." Drake orders before he covers us both with a blanket. I do as I'm told and within less than a second, his hands slide my leggings and underwear down, all the way to my knees. Fuck, what if we get caught? This is going to be humiliating.

My heart is pounding so hard.

The thought of having sex with Drake alone is enough to put me in hysteria, but put an extra dose of joining the mile high club, and it definitely gets me turned on.

I never thought I could be naughty, but hell, I have to admit this is fun. My body stills when I feel and hear Drake unzip his jeans. I almost moan when his hand strokes the back of my thighs.

Drake pulls my back against him. His heartbeat is evident against my back. I bite my lip when he whispers throatily against my ear, "Under no circumstances will you moan, scream or utter a damn word. Do we understand each other, Lil?"

I turn halfway to just see a bit of his face; when our eyes meet, I know without a doubt that I'm about to have the fucking time of my life. "Deal."

Drake kisses my shoulder as his hand starts to inch close to my mound. At this point, I'm so wet and ready for his invasion, but still, he is taking his sweet time getting to the main event. "Come here, give me your lips."

I bite my lip, twisting my head and inching closer to him, still on my side, his chest on my back. I hear him draw his breath and slowly, his lips brush against mine. The soft touch ignites something foreign inside me. I don't even wait for him to take charge. I just reach my arm up, grab the back of his head and kiss him passionately. This is Drake and I have missed him so fucking much.

His kisses are just as fevered, matching mine. I sag against him, feeling weak and dizzy. Just being in his arms again makes me feel all sorts of things; it is overwhelming. Still devouring each other's lips, his other hand snakes across and reaches inside my shirt. Pushing my bra down, his hand cups and kneads my breast. I moan against his lips when he works on my nipple, twisting and pulling it, driving me insane.

When his hand reaches lower, he stops to caress my butt in slow circles. I pull away from his lips when I feel his hand closing in on my mound, the heavenly feel is intoxicating. He slowly parts my legs, so his fingers can reach further inside. The stroke of his finger undoes me. FUCK!

"Shhhh, be quiet," Drake speaks close to my ear. His hot breath sends shivers all over my body.

His forefinger, glides up and down my womanhood. He teases my nub a few times and shocks me when he sticks a finger inside my tight hole. It's been a year since I last had sex. The alien feeling of another man touching me is too much to take. Like I said before, I suppose one could say that I am sex starved.

His finger teases as it plunges in and out of me. When he adds his thumb into the mix to rub against my clit, a soft moan escapes me.

"Lil, I warned you. Do you want me to stop?" Drake threatens.

I slightly shake my head as I grind my pussy on his hand. He takes that as a sign of understanding and I feel bereft when he withdraws his hand. He pulls my hips against his and his hard cock slides in between my thighs. I shudder at his size. *Was Drake this big the last time?* I wonder.

When I feel the head of his shaft rub against my outer core, sliding the shaft slowly, up and down to get me even wetter, I hear him warn me again in my ear. "I'm going to fuck you now, but you have to be a good girl, understood?"

"Yes," I whisper back.

With one slow, swift thrust, he slides halfway in. I turn my face on the seat to muffle my reaction. Oh God. Drake feels amazing. When his hips thrust further in, I bunch up my hands together to stop myself from screaming in pleasure. My nails bite the insides of my palm; it hurts, but I don't care. I'm past caring because what Drake is doing to me is the only thing that I can focus on. Well, it's the only thing that dominates me, nothing else matters. He grips the side of my hip so he can control the pace better.

The sweet, slow, tortured pace is driving me insane. When he goes deeper into me, my lips let out a loud gasp, but it's too late for me to take it back. Drake hisses in my ear.

I still, I'm suddenly scared he is going to stop. I sag in relief when he starts to move in and out of me again. I rejoice when his right hand snakes around my stomach and seeks my nub, rubbing it violently. My body is starting to quiver. Drake notices the sudden change in me and on cue his left hand covers my mouth while his other still touches me and his cock is still fucking me.

The forbidden feel of the whole scene, and Drake using his hand to shut me up, drives my body into such a sexual high, I come a minute after.

"Are you on the pill?" he asks, panting hard.

I shake my head, since his hand makes it impossible for me to speak. He cusses, panting like a maniac, but it doesn't stop him from pummeling me. His tongue nibbles on my earlobe. "Can I come inside you? Is it safe?"

Was it? I had my period a week and a half ago. Am I ovulating? I have no clue. It should be okay, right?

To answer his question, I push my ass hard against his cock. "Thank you." Drake's lips nip on my neck as he concentrates on his release. Then picks up pace and his finger slides around my folds, driving my body to another thrilling orgasm. His teeth painfully sink into the flesh of my neck when he unloads his semen. His small thrusts make me swell with pleasure as he pumps and drains himself inside me.

His heavy breathing tickles the back of my ear. "Did I hurt you?" he softly asks.

Yes, BUT I LOVED IT!

"No, of course not."

He kisses the spot where he sunk his teeth in hard before he pulls out of me. The instant feel of not having him connected to me makes me feel odd for some reason.

After Drake helps me with my clothing, he pulls me towards him, our faces against each other. Our eyes twinkle, obviously happy. I don't want to talk because we might just ruin the mood. Wetting my swollen lips, I slowly kiss him.

Drake pulls me closer and has my head resting against his arms as his palm cradles my face. The kiss lasts for a good forty-five minutes.

I think, in between that time, my heart starts to thaw out.

12

"I'm outside," Drake says and instantly hangs up without waiting for me to respond. We just arrived back yesterday and he woke me up an hour ago—thanks to my jet-lag, my schedule is now messed up—demanding for me to get ready. He doesn't mention where we're going.

Irritated, I grab my purse and go out the door.

What greets me is a total surprise.

Drake Tatum in black jeans, a black wife beater, black boots and straddling a black with red outlined limited edition Ducati. I stand there mesmerized at the very sight of him. His grey eyes smolder as he watches me walk towards him.

Oh, shit. I'm in so much trouble.

I haven't seen him in twenty-four hours and I'm already drooling at the sight of him. Will I be addicted to him like I was eight years ago? I better not. I don't think I'll forgive myself if I go that route again.

"Want to go for a ride?" Drake asks with a heart-thudding huskiness.

Ride.

Yes, I want to ride.

Badly.

I stride over to where he's sitting lazily on his bike and as he hands me a black helmet, I looked at him, lustfully. "I didn't know you were a biker boy." I'm wearing a short baby pink chiffon dress, how do I manage to hop on that testosterone machine?

"There's a lot about me you don't know, yet, Lil. As for your dress, just tuck it in between your legs once you're seated." Drake helps me put on the helmet. Before sliding the visor of my helmet down to shield my eyes, he stares and pauses as his eyes take me in. "You look fucking hot, Babe."

I blush and give him a shy smile that he can't see. "You look fucking delicious, too, Drake Tatum."

He gives me a toe-curling, earth-shattering, heart-attack inducing kind of smile. I blush deeper and hop on the sex-hormonal-machine. I follow his instructions and make sure I tuck the ends of my dress underneath and in between my thighs. Once I'm done, I hug him a little too tightly.

"Scared?"

Hell to the yes. "A little. Go easy on me, okay? This is my first." My voice is muffled inside the helmet.

I hear him chuckle. "I always go easy on your first times, Lil. You ought to know that by now."

My hands go inside his jacket and caress the side of his hips. I sigh at the feel of his heated, hard body. Drake takes off his helmet and seizes hold of my right hand. He kisses it before he plants it back inside his jacket. "I missed you, too, Babe," he says before he places his helmet back on and guns the bike.

If I thought Drake drove like a maniac with his sports car, he proves me wrong. The way he swerves and guns the bike is mental, coupled with insanity. It is terrifying and yet thrilling. Once in a while, he will try to reach in and squeeze my hand with his. Every time he does, my heart gives way.

I know I have to put a grinding halt to my emotions and possibly even have to end this sexual relationship I have with him, but I'm not ready, yet. Maybe, a few more days? A week? Or maybe a couple weeks, who knows? Sooner or later, though, I eventually have to end it. I can't risk losing my heart to this man. I just can't.

Once was enough.

My thoughts are dominated by him during the entire ride, I barely notice when he turns into a parking spot and kills the engine. Sure enough, I didn't even manage to read the road signs on the way, so I have no clue where we are.

I carefully hop off the bike before he does. He takes off his helmet and helps me with mine. He beams when he sees the state of my hair. "You look adorable." His fingers try to fix the mess that my hair has become. Drake being attentive and sweet is too much. When he's done, he holds the side of my jaw and kisses me. The kiss is heavy, loaded with everything that I could ask for, everything that I am scared of, and everything I have hoped for.

Lost, I am so lost in his kisses.

I'm drowning so quickly and I don't know how I can stay afloat and fight this, fight him.

When our lips part, our eyes encounter each other's as we both pant, heavily. "Where are we?" I ask, breathy and a little unstable, but I have to break that electrifying bubble we are in.

Drake grins and kisses my forehead before he responds. "Laguna Beach."

"Okay. We live around the beach. Why did we have to go an hour away to be by the beach, again?" I cock my head sideways while we leisurely stroll with the passing traffic. It is jam packed with people walking around with humming enthusiasm and excitement. Galleries, boutiques and restaurants are littered with artsy people.

"Thursdays are Art Walk. I come here whenever I get the chance, which is not very often. I wanted to show you, and at the same time, spend some time with you." Drake takes hold of my hand, entwines our fingers and acts like it's the most natural thing in the world.

"Art Walk, interesting," I state as I take in the surroundings; it's thriving and lively.

"There's a live band and art galleries are open while people, like me, drink, eat and enjoy the good things in life." Like him? Really...

"Right... because that is just your cup of tea. Right on," I tease.

But, heck, this side of him is surprising. This is definitely not the old Drake I once knew. This is the neo-Drake that I have yet to get to know. I have to admit that I like the new him.

It's endearing to see him relaxed with me. We go to one gallery after the other and another. It is endless. Drake is jovial while we both discuss art and what he loves most about it. We're walking past a handmade jewelry boutique when he tugs my hand, which brings me to stop. "What?"

"Let's go check this place out." He points his head towards the store and leads the way.

It's a tiny store, but it consists of some pretty intricate handmade items. I'm checking out ankle bracelets when I see Drake purchase something. Shrugging, I stroll to the other side of the store and admire a few more delicate necklaces.

"Like anything?" Drake asks from behind me.

Like I would tell him if I liked something? I don't plan for him to pay for the things I want. I can do it myself.

I shake my head. "Nope, nothing catches my eye, yet." I spin around and smile at him. "What did you get? A man bracelet? Something for your mom?"

Drake's forefinger strokes the base of my neck. The light brush simply burns me. "I got something for you. Turn around." I do as he asks, pulling my long dark hair to the side of my shoulder. Drake slowly places a delicate gold star necklace around my neck, making sure to delicately swipe his fingers across the back of my neck. It brings out an involuntary shiver. "There, now. It looks perfect on you."

Melt me more, Drake, because by the end of the night, there will be no resolve left in me. "A star? It's cute and pretty. I didn't know you liked them. Thank you." I give him a lingering kiss.

"I'm not much of a star person, but I thought it'd be something to remember me by." Drake kisses my forehead and takes my hand.

We leave the store in a light mood. I'm surprised when Drake pulls me in a small corner, away from the crowd. "It was stars you stared at when I took you the first time. It's a token for that magical night. I remember everything about it like it was just yesterday. The way you looked, smelled, felt under my touch. I have never forgotten you. You were the ghost that haunted my thoughts and dreams. I'm done thinking and dreaming, I want to live it . . . with you."

I swallow whatever saliva I have left in the sudden dryness of my throat. "But you didn't want me. You left the next day. You sent me away when I went to visit you. You didn't want me . . ." I trail off as my memories relive those gut-wrenching moments.

Drake looks away and studies the pavement. "I've always wanted you. I just didn't want to be tied down with such a big, fucking commitment. At that age, all I wanted to do was party and date around. If I pursued you, our parents would've expected us to be engaged and married the minute we got out of college. I wasn't ready for marriage."

Me? A big commitment? If we had just communicated, we could've at least worked something out, but then, I guess he wanted to date other women, too. So, I suppose that won out for him.

I press my lips together and try to smile. It's hard to do so when my heart feels heavy. "Well, I guess you made the right decision. It was for the best." Drake just studies me closely.

The heavy scrutiny makes me uncomfortable.

Pushing off from the side of the building, I drag him towards the crowd. I don't want to talk about the past. Nothing good ever comes out of it. I get it. He didn't want to be with me back then. I don't need to keep rehashing it twice a day. It's taxing and most importantly, I'm sick of it.

I'm done talking about it.

After half an hour listening to the live band playing, we decide to have dinner in one of the restaurants nearby.

After the waiter takes our orders, I go check my messages, as does he. I'm texting Masie, my best friend, when my phone suddenly starts ringing.

Jared.

I glance over at Drake who is busy with emails. "I'll be back," I inform him as I get up and go around to where the bathrooms are located. It's the quietest area I can find.

"Jared?"

"I was just about to hang up. How are you? How was Greece? Have some crazy fun under the sun?" Jared teases as he laughs lightly.

His niceness makes me feel like a heel. "It was great fun. How are you?" I ask, changing the subject and directing the conversation back towards him.

Certainly my life is chaotic at the moment. Glossing over it doesn't feel right, either.

"I'm great! I'm actually excited to see you again. Do you have any idea when you'll let me come over?" Jared's tone just became serious.

I know he is referring more to my answer to his question about taking our relationship to another level, than actually coming over. It's been a year since I've been in a relationship and Jared fits the bill for the kind of guy that I usually go for. I did want to make things work with him before I left for Greece . . . before Drake and I happened.

I know Drake and I won't last. The past is just too much of a cloud to make things easy for us. Besides, he just broke up with Shannon. Drake isn't the forever after type; he may want me now, but that will wear off. Men like Drake always want variety. So, that leaves me with one option and that is to stop this thing with Drake before I decide things with Jared.

I've been seeing Jared for ten weeks now, on and off with casual dates here and there. I like Jared. "How about tomorrow night? You get to pick."

"That's my girl. I'll pick you up around seven?"

I smile. Yeah, I'm making the right decision. "Seven it is. See you!" I hang up the phone and stride towards our table.

Silently, I sit across Drake. Each movement is being studied and analyzed. I take a lengthy sip of my water.

"Was that Jared?" Drake shoots the question directly.

I bite the inside of my cheek before I nod my head. Why is he so nosy, anyway?

"What did he want?" he presses on.

"We spoke for a bit. This and that." Vague? Yeah, very much so.

Drake glares at me. "This and that? Did you tell him that you're with me now? That you're not an available woman?" he asks through gritted teeth.

That, certainly amps up my temper. "I am nobody's woman. Yet."

His nostrils flare as his jaws lock together. "You better watch it, Lil. I don't want to make a scene to prove a point."

I'm sure.

The waiter brings our food. I've already lost my appetite, so I barely pick at my food. Drake doesn't seem too keen on his, either. Cussing, he pushes his plate aside, gets up and places twice the amount of our bill on the table.

"Outside, Lil. We need to talk. NOW," Drake bites out before he leaves the restaurant, his face is dark with anger.

13

I'm nervous as hell when I walk out of the restaurant and find him close to where he parked his Ducati, leaning against the tree trunk, arms folded against his chest while he watches me walk over to him.

"We fucked yesterday. Did that mean anything to you?" he hisses at me.

Whoa, he doesn't waste time getting to the point. Did it mean something to me? Yeah, it did, of course, but was it enough to lose my head over? No. "Well . . . I thought it was just . . . sex."

Drake makes an evil, cruel laugh. "Sex. Just sex." He laughs again. "I don't fucking believe this. Lily Alexander, of all women, I would've never thought you would fuck just to fuck. I guess I was too caught up seeing and being with you again. I was alone in this it seems."

Okay, that stings a little bit. "I . . ." I open my mouth and close it. I was what? Sorry? But I'm not sorry.

Drake swiftly stands close to me. "You what, Lil?" he questions bitingly in my ear.

"Can we just forget about it? It was only once." I see him flinch. His eyes cloud over, chilling with temper.

Drake looks at me like he's seeing me for the first time. I know for a fact that he doesn't like what he's seeing. I'm not naively strung out on love and adoration for him. I've changed. He can't just expect me to throw everything out the window just because the ever elusive Drake Tatum decided to pursue me, us, together. After a minute of him still in a state of silence, I'm starting to panic. I suddenly wet my dry lips as my mind stampedes on.

When he speaks again, I tremble. "Let me fuck you tonight. Then you can go."

I gasp at his proposition. Was that even sensible? We're too heightened with tension.

One more night . . . in his arms . . . one more night.

"Just tonight?" I double check, arching my eyebrow at him.

"Just tonight." Drake looks determined and detached.

Gone is the Drake from earlier. The Drake before me now, is the Drake I knew so well, a mercurial, insufferable, enthralling, dominating, blasted kind of a man.

=====

During the ride back, gone were the light touches and hand soothing gestures. Drake was detached and stone cold. When we arrive outside his house in Malibu, Drake stops and takes out his gate remote. His home, Italian style meets contemporary design, comes into view. It's a rectangular villa made with limestone and bricks. His driveway is lit with embedded, small, circled-lights along the pathway. The only word that comes to mind is *stunning*.

What I immediately notice is that his house is surrounded with a lot of wild blooms as well as an overabundance of lavender. The smell of lavender along with the smell of the ocean is rather intoxicating. The three-car garage door is stained and brushed to perfection in order to look rustic and Spartan. Old civilization meets contemporary. It was done in such a perfect blend of colors that it works beautifully, matching its owner.

Once inside the garage, Drake parks right next to his sports car and kills the engine. I release my arms from around him and get off the bike. I try to unlatch the strap around my helmet, but have a hard time doing so.

Fuck, I cuss inside my head. *I hate helmets!*

Drake, who already took off his, pulls me close to him and helps me with it. He is still on his bike, both legs apart, feet on the floor. He eyes me predatorily. Drake is simply sinful as he smolders. The dangerous vibe that emanates from him only gets me more excited.

"What?" I ask. My eyes devouring him.

"Lily."

Drake's eyes are dilated when he roughly pulls me against his thigh and captures my lips. His kiss is punishing, no holds bar as he obliterates my lips. It's passionate, greedy, fervent and ardent with each kiss. I'm being consumed with no reservations. Moaning, I place my hands on the back of his head, locking it against mine. My world tilts as our tongues spar ferociously.

I want him so fucking much. My head chants it over and over, driving me insane.

Like I weigh nothing, Drake lifts me up and places me on the bike facing him with my legs on each side of the bike, sitting above his thighs.

His hands are all over me, caressing and probing. Still kissing me, his hands hastily slide the shoulder straps of my dress off, pushing it down just enough to expose my breasts. I'm breathless when his hands work their magic on my nipples. Both thumbs and fingers pinch, twist and pull in amazing synchronization.

"Drake," I draw his name out with a whisper, panting.

His lips then seek my earlobe and nip all the way down to the base of my throat as his hands are still doing their delicious ministrations.

"You drive me so crazy, but I can't get enough of you. God, help me. I just can't." Drake places me on my back, on the gas tank, before he takes one erect nipple in his mouth.

God help me, indeed.

I arch my body more towards him, his mouth, and his hands while I tug at his hair every time he playfully bites my pebbled nipples. An animalistic growl comes from him. With enough force, Drake yanks my dress off my body, ripping it like it's a piece of paper. My lips hang ajar as I look at my almost naked body, then look to the ripped dress that he carelessly flung on the floor.

"Open your legs wide," Drake orders.

I only have my black lacy thong on. I plant my soles on both of his thighs. My legs are a little shaky when I part them to the furthest they can go.

Using his middle finger, he traces the outline of my thong, right over the folds of my sex. I shiver as I watch him with utmost concentration. His finger nudges the soft elastic to the side and his eyes lift, meeting my gaze. His lips are slightly parted, eyes simply fascinated. He is deliberately stroking me, in such a slow, turtle-paced speed I'm starting to get angry at the tease. "Arch towards me."

I do as he asks while his slow-paced finger doesn't accelerate at all. Drake bites the side of my breast as his middle finger punishingly strikes inside my entrance. I yelp at his crass invasion. The garage ceiling starts to spin above me to the motion of his finger. Drake is rough on me. I didn't mention that I haven't had sex in a year, well besides for when we were on the airplane. I'm wet, yes, but still, it stings.

Drake doesn't even give me any indication when he suddenly rips of my thin, lacy thong while his finger is at its own mission. Twisting his wrist, his thumb fervently rubs against my core. My body starts to quake, my breasts shaking, and my back arching as I greedily ask for more. "Ahh, Drake . . ." I bite my lip as I moan his name.

He pulls out of me and shockingly sticks half of his middle finger inside my mouth. Our eyes connect. "Suck your juices off my finger." Slowly, I suck, all the way to the base of it and up again while I watch him through my lashes.

"You look so wild and abandoned. I could nut just watching you like that." I lick my lips when I see him take off his leather jacket and hastily place it behind me. When he takes his shirt off and dumps it next to my ripped dress, there is no going back. I hungrily eye him. His hands skim the sides of my thighs, all the way down, to my ankle. Like a pro, he grabs my ankles and slides my body down towards him. Strong arms lift my legs onto his shoulders before his mouth ravages my inner core.

His hot invasion heats me further. Clutching his thighs, my nails dig through his jeans when he stabs his tongue in and out of me while his hands toy with my breasts.

I have no idea where I get the strength to balance my body in that peculiar position. I have never realized how flexible I am until now. Drake demolishes me with his tongue and fingers. My body tenses when my orgasm peaks. I scream his name like it's my fucking salvation.

I'm sweating and panting hard when he comes up for air. "I'm going to destroy this nice, little, tight pussy, Babe. You won't be able to move for a few days without hurting. Each time you do, you'll be reminded how I tore this up." When Drake searches for my lips, I am beyond dizzy.

I'm in a sexual trance. I am hooked, high and flying.

He gently places me back down while he cautiously gets up, unbuckles his pants and slides them down, mid-thigh. His thick, ready to combust, cock catches my attention. The head is thick and fat. The silken length lined with pronounced veins. Everything about this man demands attention. Even his manhood is a sight to behold.

How the heck did he manage to get that in the last couple of times? I wonder.

He sits back down, his cock positioned upwards stiffly. Drake gathers me in his arms. I wind my arms around him, as he places my legs over his thighs. My sex is pressed against his hard, hot length while we make out again. I cry out when Drake breaks our kiss and trails his mouth across my jaw to my earlobe.

"Do you want me?" he whispers against my ear while he grabs ahold of his cock and pats it against my wet mound.

"Drake . . . I . . . want you . . ." I'm under his mercy. There's no doubt about that.

"How much?" he angrily asks.

I know he is referring to our conversation from earlier in Laguna Beach, but I'm past caring. At this point, I will say yes to anything. "Very much."

"Go ahead. Take as much as you want. Ride this cock until you can't take it anymore. I want you to have your turn to enjoy it because, once you're done, I will take as much pleasure as I can from this tight cunt. My cock will own, burn, sting and fucking mark you. You will not be the same woman."

God, dirty talk, plus Drake . . . Kill me now. It's so fucking sexy.

He hastily lifts my hips and positions me above the head of his shaft. Calmly, I lower my body and stop when the tip hits the spot right outside my entrance. With one hand on his shoulder, I snake the other down to seek out his length. I hear him hiss when I gently stroke it. I slowly rub my wet folds over it again and again.

"Oh, God! You feel so good," I cry out in pleasure.

When I can't take it anymore, I gently press my hips down. The head of his shaft slips inside me. "Fuck, baby. Don't tighten around my cock like that or I'm not going to last long. Ease up a bit."

I'll try.

Using slow motions, I start to acclimatize to his length and girth. He's not even halfway in and it already feels full. "Baby! Fuck! Are you okay?"

I bite my lip, unsure. "Yeah, it's just . . . it's been a year and half since I last had sex, before you. It's taking a little longer for me to get used to it, I guess."

Drake smiles, surely pleased. "You have no idea how that pleases me. Do you trust me, babe?"

I nod. "Yes," I whisper before Drake captures my lips, barely half of his cock inside me. His thumb manically rubs my core, stimulating me more. When it is dripping with wetness, he asks me again if I trust him. I whispered yes and capture his lips again.

His large hands caress my back. Both hands grip my ass cheeks so tightly. I moan in between kisses. He slaps my left cheek, hard. I yelp against his lips. I'm so focused on the hot stinging pain of my skin that I don't notice him hold my hips and push them down his thick length. All the way down.

"Drake!" I sob as the hellish raw sting of his cock wreaks havoc on my body. My nails dig through the skin of his shoulder.

"Shhh . . . it's over now." Drake tries to soothe me.

His cock is huge. Inside me, it feels monstrous. Getting back in position, I start to move gently.

"Does it still hurt?" he asks as he starts to rub my mound.

"A bit." I close my eyes and focus on his cock. After a few times of sliding it in and out of me, the pleasure overpowers the burning sting. If it's possible for him to get any bigger, it does.

It simply adds to my pleasure.

"Better?" he asks and I simply nod. My body starts to demand more and so I up my speed, riding him. "I'm going to get us inside, but don't stop fucking me. Hold on, tight."

It's difficult to move my hips while he gets us inside the house, but I manage. We enter the garage door that leads inside his home. The second we get inside, Drake slams me against the wall.

"Forgive me, but I have to take you. Right now." Drake doesn't even give me a chance to respond because he starts fucking me against the wall so hard that I become like a rag doll, limp in his arms and thrust around. Within seconds, I'm coming apart and I scream so loud, his house echoes for a while with my high-pitched screams. "Wrap your legs around me. I'm going to fuck you harder."

Harder?

Yes, harder.

Lightning speed hard. My orgasm is weaving through me while I scream his name in vain, over and over again. Drake joins me, barking my name out before he unloads his semen inside my womb. He makes little, tense thrusts while he rides out his own orgasm.

Breathless, Drake wipes the damp hair off my forehead, pushing it aside as his eyes seek mine. His cock twitches inside me. Something flashes in his eyes, but before I catch it, he lowers his head and kisses me softly.

This kiss feels entirely different . . . personal, somehow.

The longer we kiss, the more his cock starts to awaken again and pulsates to life. I'm ready to go for round two right here, but he sweeps us upstairs. When we pass his bed, I protest. "Bed, please. I want it on the bed this time."

He laughs and slaps my ass hard again. He slowly pulls out of me and gently places me on the floor in the bathroom. My legs are shaky, but I manage to stand and not fall on my face. Drake turns on the whirlpool tub and fills it with lavender bath oil. The water is still running when he hoists me up and carefully places me inside the large tub. Drake jumps in behind me and gathers me in his arms. I sag against his hard torso. *Perfection,* I think with alarming satisfaction.

Please, don't make me fall for him again.

"This feels nice," I murmur against his chest.

"Did I hurt you? I don't know if you noticed, but there was a little blood." His fingers are gently touching my arm, stroking it mindlessly. I barely notice.

"It did in the beginning, but I'm just sore now." I feel butterflies flutter about in my stomach when Drake murmurs sweet nothings while he massages my shoulders, kissing them from time to time.

I sigh, contently. "That feels so good. Please, don't stop." I purr when I feel his cock harden against my back.

Drake's mouth starts to make its way around the curve of my neck while one hand is on my breast, the other starts to part my folds. Damn, I want him again.

When my hand reaches out behind me to stroke his length, he moves it away. "Relax and enjoy. I was selfish earlier. We still have a long night ahead of us."

Hmm, I wonder what his plans are . . .

After Drake makes me come again in the tub, I'm beyond spent. He plucks me out of the tub, half asleep, as he wipes me down with a fluffy towel. He then whisks me off to his bed and tucks me in, naked.

It's the last thing I remember before sleep catches up with me.

14

Something wakes me up, but it feels too good, soothingly good, it puts me back to sleep. I moan when I feel a tongue circle my entrance.

"Drake," I utter, somewhat asleep.

I feel him slowly come up towards me through my parted legs and claim my lips. "Didn't mean to wake you . . . but it's hard to resist temptation when you're so close in my reach," he says in between kisses. I love how his body presses against mine as he kisses me. His lips go for my neck, soft kisses almost putting me back to sleep.

"Babe?"

I merely grunt. What now? I'm still jet-lagged and my body is still reeling from it.

Why isn't he tired?

"Is it okay if I just . . . do whatever I want with your body?" Drake asks, using his uber-hot bedroom voice.

Like I'm going to dream of declining that offer.

"Whatever, go ahead. I'm going back to sleep." I barely get my response out when he demolishes my lips.

Again.

I happily smile when he breaks our kiss. His lips trail lower, back to where he was earlier. The way his tongue strokes and probes, it's somehow gentle and calming . . . but fucking good. I have no idea how long he eats me out because I'm going in and out of my sleeping state, but I do wake up when the head of his cock pushes at my entrance as he slowly thrusts all the way in, hitting the very depths of me.

"You're so tight, you push me back out. I fucking love it. I love everything about you." Drake obsesses about me being tight. His breathing, ragged against my neck, before he rams inside my sore entrance again.

I'm gasping for air when he hammers it into me with such force that I think I'm seeing stars. His hands lift my hips, gaining more access, deepening within me.

I tighten at the odd sensation. "Oh my, you're hitting the wall of my cervix." I'm not sure if I like it or not. It just feels weird.

"Open your legs wider. I want more of you." He commands and I nervously follow suit.

Drake is definitely bossy and dominating in bed, but who doesn't like a man who knows that he's The Boss? It's such a turn on.

"The more I fuck you like this, the easier it will become. You just need to adjust and get used to my size," he speaks in between thrusts, against my lips. "It's fucked up that I'm getting more aroused, knowing you're this tight. The thought of me stretching you until you can't take any more of my size, gets me so damn hard. You feel like a virgin, just like that night, tight as a glove around me, as it suctions my cock back into this unused hole."

Lord, help me.

"I'm not going to stop you. I love . . ." I cry out when he starts to pummel me harder.

"You love what?" he asks in between kisses.

Fuck.

I fucking love him.

Still.

After all these years, it is still there, sitting, biding its time until I free it again.

"You drive me crazy. I can't get enough of you," I confess a different truth. Drake need not know the other one.

He takes me hard and fast. I come and almost pass out. Drake is still coming. I notice that he didn't use condoms again. It's the third time. I really have to remember to speak to him about that.

I'm a blink away from sleep when he kisses my chest, panting. He pushes his cock a few more times. "I hope I'm not too late."

Shit.

I try to control my breathing because I somehow know that Drake thinks I'm fast asleep. His face is in between my breasts. My heart stops when I hear him again. "I love you. It's always been you."

Double shit.

That can't be true because if he did love me all this time, he could've called or visited me, but he didn't do any of those things. In fact, he simply didn't do anything.

No, it's not love. He's just high on sex hormones.

=====

"Wake up!" Drake nuzzles his nose on the back of my head. His arms held me all night.

"How could you ask me to do that when you kept waking me up so many times last night that I lost count?" I grumble.

I flinch when I feel my overused muscles down south. Shit, it still stings.

When I feel his manhood harden against my back, I'm ready to throw in the towel. "I'm sore. You have to wait."

He rolls on top of me, grinning. "I did warn you."

Yeah, he did.

I thought he was just joking. He puts the word insatiable to shame. Drake looks happy. I suppose those orgasms did a good job.

"Stay the entire weekend with me. I already called in sick for both of us." He suddenly looks unsure. "Just you and me..."

Three more days with Drake . . . that spells disaster of epic proportion.

Jared. Fuck, I'm supposed to meet him for dinner.

"Okay, I could do that, but I have to do something really quick tonight. Then, I'll just drive out here. I . . ."

"You've got yourself a deal woman." Drake's eyes twinkle as he looks down on me smiling.

"What?" I ask at his grinning face.

He shakes his head. "I just realized how awesome it is waking up with you in bed."

Oh.

"That's . . . nice," I finally manage to respond after a few seconds of pausing.

"What time do you have to leave?" Drake lightly inquires while his eyes rove over my slightly exposed breasts. He is clearly already distracted.

My breasts are raw and sensitive from his fondling last night, but that doesn't seem to stop him. I'm relieved when he just uses his tongue, flicking them with it, while his eyes look at me squarely, waiting for me to answer his question.

Crazy man. "I'm hoping to leave around five, and then I'll be back tonight."

"Good, good," Drake whispers as he lowers himself in between my parted thighs.

I tense. Oh, my, freaking gods! When will he stop?!

"Drake! No! I'm sore!" I squawk, out of breath.

The man gives me a wicked smile as he lifts both legs and places them on his back. "I'm just going to eat you out . . . nothing more, nothing less . . . Well, unless . . . you want to do other things, that is. Then, I'm up for it."

"But . . ." I linger as the first touch of his tongue delves in between my folds. The ministrations are soft and hot, but he executes with such precision it is mind-numbing. Goodness! Is this his specialty? Likely . . .

"Drake! Drake!" I bellow, my hand clutching a bunch of his hair as I press my hips against his expert mouth.

My body tightens. My vaginal muscles clench, anticipating release. I half sit-up, loving the sight of Drake in between my legs; it arouses me more than ever. He jolts me when he instantly shakes his head, making his tongue flick back and forth in my wet core.

His eyes dare me to let go and I'm getting there . . . almost at the finish line. I hear him groan when his hands lift my hips and his fingertips grip my ass.

Fucking. Hell. I pant, watching him as my breasts shake from the small quakes that my body is going through. "Give it to me . . . I'm almost there . . ." I beg and beg.

His right middle finger goes underneath his tongue, gathering my wetness in circular motions. I arch my torso with my hands planted straight behind my back as I stare at the ceiling. I bite my lip when I feel that finger slide down on that small line in between my pussy and my anus. That finger teases the sensitive line. My body is set on fire when it slides lower, rubbing my backdoor entrance with determined purpose.

"Fuck! Drake!" I protest when his mouth leaves my pussy.

"Kiss me," he whispers, while I blink a few times. His finger is making me feel... "Kiss. Me. Now," Drake demands, his eyes flashing. With no patience, he pulls my neck and kisses me mercilessly. "Hang on, tight, Babe," he tells me before he inserts two fingers inside my wet core.

I am under his spell. Whatever this is with Drake, I am so deep in it. I have no clue how to come out alive and in one piece.

"Hang on tight." Drake's eyes watch me as those fingers of his frenetically, relentlessly capture my G-spot and hold it ransom. "Come for me,

Baby. That's my girl," he commands. It's cruel, mind-blowing and fucking beautiful.

Yes, beautiful. The crushing tidal wave of my screams as my cataclysmic orgasm surges forth and ripple all over my limp body. It's so powerful that I have tears in my eyes.

My body is still riding the aftershocks when Drake pulls me into his arms, stroking my hair, he asks, "How are you feeling? You look traumatized." He gives a small chuckle.

Traumatized, my ass. I am borderline mental and halfway paralyzed. "What the hell was that?" I wonder out loud.

He kisses my forehead. "That, my dear, is what I call a sublime orgasm."

Sublime orgasm, seriously? "Is that what you specialize in, or something?"

He might be right about traumatized though . . . I am when it comes to him. Does he realize how long it took me to get over his rejection? Two whole years. I didn't date until I was twenty. How many women has he done this to? How can a woman move on after him, after this kind of life-altering, blissful perfection? I know I'm fucked already. Good luck to me, trying to move forward. Sooner or later, I will eventually give Drake up, but it will be done with wrenching difficulty.

"Think of the perks you can get being with me. I'm not a selfish lover. I actually love seeing your entire body blush and sweat profusely from my tongue alone."

Right . . . why don't I just lose my head in the process . . . since my heart is already unsalvageable? Why don't we just add that on top on the shit list?

I keep my mouth shut in case I end up saying something I will regret. Funny . . . eight days . . . It took only eight days for me to realize that I'm still in love with Drake. After eight years of loathing the man, I just succumb and crumble the second he kisses me.

Drake taught me a lot of things. How to be angry, bitter, insecure, ugliness, rejection and I can go on and on . . . I suppose, since I am in the shitter, the only thing I can do is be smart with what I tell him. Confessing my ever-lasting love to him is out of the question. I just have to be guarded is all.

I try to move out of his arms, needing space, but he catches my hand, stopping me.

Drake frowns as he watches my demeanor change. "Where are you going? It's not five yet?"

"Shower, do you mind?"

Drake tries to look unoffended by my sudden aloofness, but it's not all that hard to see. "Can I share that with you?" he asks lightly.

"Drake . . . I need space . . . you're all over the place. I need some space to think."

He nods. Without saying a word, he lets go of me. I sag in confusion before I let myself in the bathroom and take a lengthy, hot shower.

=====

I am in the shower for almost an hour. I guess, one can say, I am more than troubled. Since, I don't have any clothes, any panties or dress to speak of; I hunt for a shirt in Drake's closet.

His walk-in closet is very masculine. Dark cherry wood with a lot of chrome on black carpet covers most of the design. I almost faint at the smell of the large expanse of room. Drake's smell permeates the air. My eyes take in all of his clothes and knick-knacks. Different ties, watches and shoes are all displayed in shades. He wasn't kidding when he mentioned his thing about color coordination. I walk towards a set of drawers and find a large Columbia shirt. I take it out and put it on, then gather my wet hair and bunch it together, making it into a haphazard wet bun. I stride out of his closet and pause. Across from me is another closed door.

Curiosity wins out and I find myself opening the door and flicking the light switch on. I find myself on Shannon's turf. It's easy to see that she's gathered some of her things rather quickly because she still left a lot behind. The size of the closet is the same as Drake's, but hers is much more feminine. The woman must love purple, a lot, because the closet is full of the color. I cautiously walk in, stopping a foot away from the center table and accessory drawer. On it is a smashed picture frame of them together. They're in a formal setting, possibly a party. Drake is kissing her as Shannon gazes at the camera, happy and obviously in love.

I stare at them as emotions roll through me. Was I ever that happy with another man? I've had three serious boyfriends and they were all great, but I don't think I was as happy or blissful as the picture portrays. Shannon radiates it. Drake looks smitten, too. Well, I guess, they were in love. I mean, they did plan to get married before Drake broke it off.

Am I his rebound? Tears gather up in my eyes as I look around Shannon's things. This house is theirs. They have memories in this place.

I don't know what hurts more; seeing Drake happy with another woman, or that he almost married and had a baby with her. This was the real deal, right here. I better snap out of my love haze before I fall flat on my face.

Wiping my tears away, I look for Drake. I want to go home, but I don't have a car to drive home with. Instead of solid walls, his house has a large expanse of thick tinted glass. It overlooks the Pacific Ocean, but unlike mine, his is on a cliff with a large rectangular pool and a Jacuzzi. The chic white outlines with black cabanas are a pretty posh addition.

It's sick, but I can't help seeing Shannon everywhere I look around this house.

Mocking me.

"Drake?" I call out to the eerie silence of the house. Where the hell did that man go now?

When I get to the kitchen, I find a note. Going to Mom's to get Skull. He stayed there while we were in Greece. I will be back soon. Miss you. ~ D

Sighing, I wander towards the garage door. I'm surprised that none of my things are on the floor. Where is my purse? I need my phone.

I find my purse on top of the bar in his living room. I hit speed dial without blinking. When I hear my call being picked up, I rapidly speak, "I need your help. I don't have a ride or clothes for that matter, so I can't call for a cab without humiliating myself. I need you to pick me up in Malibu . . . at Drake's house."

Masie whistles. "Got yourself in trouble, Miss Goody? Fine, I'll fish out the details later. Text me the address and I will be there to pick you up and watch you do the walk of shame. I hope last night was worth it, sweetie." She sounds worried. I would be, too, if the situation was reversed.

I give her my thanks and send her Drake's address. It's good to have a friend to count on through this, but Masie and her boyfriend, Nick, both like Jared, a lot. I'm going to catch a lot of hell over this walk of shame.

Jared. I'll be seeing him tonight. I have to get my shit together because I have to make a decision.

15

"Jared!" I greet him at the door before he gathers me in his arms and kisses me on the lips.

That definitely surprises me. Sure, we've kissed and fooled around, but it never goes further than that.

After leaving Drake's home, feeling dejected and with my insecurity at the highest level, I decide to dress up a little. I wear a nude, tight-fitting corset dress that my lithe body and legs look amazing in paired with my sand colored Prada platform pumps to finish the look. I look pretty decent, if I do say so myself. I straightened my usually wavy hair. I forgot how changing hairstyles actually does wonders to a woman's look alone. I keep my make-up light, but don't hold back with my scarlet lipstick.

No more Drake, I can't think about him tonight with Jared. Jared deserves my undivided attention. It also helps that Drake hasn't tried to call me or text. It hurts that he can't bother to send me even a quick text; yet, I'm relieved that he doesn't. Fucking confusing. I want to scream my frustration.

Jared steps back. His eyes heatedly admire my look as he whistles. "You look like a supermodel. I know you're gorgeous and all, but you never used to dress up this way for me."

I blush and murmur my thanks. A big part of me is pleased that there is a guy out there that appreciates my efforts.

Yeah, I was pretty laid back before. I guess Jared can thank Drake for making me feel like shit. After I found that picture of him and Shannon, I couldn't get it out of my head. Jared is a good-looking guy. Six-feet tall with a well-honed body, wavy blonde hair, light brown eyes and armed with a charming, amiable personality.

"Where are we going?" I ask before I get my things and start heading out the door.

Jared looks at me, grinning. "Well, since you're asking, it's actually my parents' thirty-fifth wedding anniversary. They're having this bash at their house. I'm taking you there as my date."

I can feel my body grow taut. "You want me to meet your parents?" I ask in a whisper.

"Don't freak out, okay? I just thought since you're deciding if you want to seriously date me, and be exclusive . . . I want to show you where I come from. Of course, I want Mom and Dad to meet you. It's only a party. It's nothing to be scared of. Well, I hope they don't scare you away." He looks thoughtful for a moment.

"I'm not scared, Jared. You just caught me by surprise, that's all." It's more like I'm feeling along the lines of a slut because I spent all night having sex with Drake and here comes Jared, sweet and perfect, wanting to introduce me to his parents.

Jared kisses the top of my nose. "You'll be fine. You're great. You're perfect. Well, I think you're perfect, anyway."

Shit. Just shit, fuck, shit, shit, shit.

The ride to his parents' home in Calabasas is pretty engaging. Jared is studying to be a doctor in cardiology and he's passionate about it. He'll be doing his residency program at UCLA medicine soon. Jared is actually friends with Nick. I had declined Jared's invitation for a whole year before I finally decided to give him a shot. Now, exactly when I realize I'm ready to move forward, Drake happens to show back up in my life.

It's fucked up.

Jared glances at me before he reaches out to give my bare thigh a tight squeeze. His hand stays there, unmoving, just there. "Masie mentioned that you two are planning on opening a business?"

"Since, she and I have this obsession with cupcakes and we loved making them in college, we thought . . . well, why not go for it? It hasn't been finalized yet, though. We need to look for a location first, and then go from there."

His hand hasn't moved, but his fingers are stroking my skin, back and forth. "Your cupcakes are delicious. I can't get enough of them." His voice lowers, full of innuendo.

Um, is he still talking about cupcakes here? The way he mentions them . . . it sounded downright sexual.

When my phone rings, I decide to get it. It's Mom. "Hey! What's up, Mom?"

"How are you, Dear? I'm actually calling to tell you that Patricia is having a luncheon this Sunday. I was hoping you would come." Mom sounds nervous.

Weird, why would she be nervous? "Sure. Is that all because I'm getting the vibe that there's more?"

Mom clears her throat. "There is . . . but I'm not sure if telling you over the phone is the best way to tell you."

There is no way in Hell I am letting my mother off the phone without telling me. "It is, actually. My mind is going through the scenarios right now and I would greatly appreciate it if you would relieve me of that kind of tension."

"Fine, if you insist. I'm seeing someone. I started dating again." Huh? Since when did she start dating?

For the last nine years, Mom never even mentioned another guy. So, I had assumed that she wasn't dating. When did that change?

"Who are you dating?" I am in shock.

"Colin Sandberg"

Oh, Hell. He's a close friend of Hugh's and had been very close with my dad when he was alive, too.

"Lily? Will you say something?" Mom is waiting for my reaction. What the heck do I say?

"Um, that was unexpected. I didn't realize you were attracted to Colin. He's Dad's friend, Mom. I don't know. How long have you been seeing him?"

"A week ago. It just started. He said he finally manned up and asked me out. He's been meaning to for the last few years, but always hesitated." That sounds like Colin.

Colin Sandberg is a decent man, gentle and soft-spoken with the sharpest brain around. His wife died five years ago, I think. He doesn't have any children because his wife didn't want any, but they were happy that way. It was a lifestyle choice that suited them both. I suppose two lonely grieving people are entitled to find solace in each other.

"I'm happy for you, Mom. I really am. Colin better not hurt you or he'll have me to answer to." My mother chuckles at that. She knows I can be a spitfire about it, too; if it ever comes down to that.

I honestly hope that it won't. Mom deserves to be happy. I hadn't realized how lonely she must be since Dad died.

"That's why I called, too. Colin will be joining us this Sunday. That's why it's important that you come."

That warms my heart. Mom. Introducing her boyfriend for the first time. Ha! "Of course, count me in. Lunch, right?"

"Yes, I will see you then. Have a goodnight, Hon."

"You, too, Mom," I say before we part with our goodbyes.

I glance sideways and find Jared looking amused. "Glad my mom's love life entertains you, Mr. Pearson."

"It is a bit entertaining, but I think your love life intrigues me more." He gives my thigh another stroke.

I weave myself nicely on a nice shit pile, don't I?

"I'm sure it does," I murmur. Not wanting to open that can of worms. Drake, our past and the ever shifting present, are not what I want to talk or even think about tonight.

My phone beeps to indicate a text message.

Drake.

My heart rate suddenly speeds up, I feel suffocated.

What time will you be here tonight? I forgot to ask. Miss you, Lil.

Do I still want to do this weekend thing with Drake? I do and don't, but after I saw that picture of him and Shannon together, I don't think I can do it. Hell, but the thought of having a crazy sex-fest with Drake all weekend long makes me break out with goose bumps.

I decide to text Drake back, right then and there. It's best I get it over with before I meet Jared's parents because that is a major deal for me.

Hey . . . I don't think that will be possible, Drake. Let's just try to move past what happened the last few days? If it's possible . . . I would really appreciate it. I'll see you at work Monday. Thanks.

There. I sent it. The message sounds rational and mature. When it beeps again, I shove it back in my purse. There's no point in trying to ruin my night. Drake can wait.

=====

Mr. and Mrs. Pearson welcome me with such warmth and enthusiasm that it makes me feel guilty as hell.

Why? Drake, of course.

Abby and Warren Pearson are the epitome of soul-mates, if such a thing does exist, these two would be on the top roster. Jared has his father's structure and facial features, but he has his mother's eyes and smile.

The party for their wedding anniversary probably has about three hundred guests. It's chaotic, crazy and lively with happy chatters. It is, after all, a celebration of love. Thirty-five years of it.

Their sprawling lush garden has been transformed into a beautiful setting of white, more white, and a hint of dark purple. Each time we pass a person, Jared greets them genuinely and everyone seems pleased to meet me.

I'm seated with Jared and the rest of his relatives, which there are many of them; I have a hard time remembering their names.

"So, this is the woman that finally captured my brother's heart?" a guy says from behind me. When he comes into view, he smiles with an outstretched hand. "I'm Jared's brother, Jason."

"Lily Alexander." I take his outstretched hand and shake it.

Jason looks like Jared, except he has green eyes. If I didn't know any better, I could mistake them for twins. Jason is younger by two years, though. So, when he decides to join us at our table, I prepare myself for the mini interrogation that I'm sure is coming.

Instead, I get a whole lot of laughs. Jared and Jason together are definitely crazy fun. They joke like they are best friends. There is no sibling rivalry to speak of. Eventually everyone becomes quiet when Warren stands up with a microphone.

"Ladies and gentlemen, I just want to thank all of you for coming here to celebrate this tremendously special day with us. Thirty-five years of happiness with my Abby. Yes, people. Staying married can be done." People laugh at that, as do I. Jared reaches out for my hand and kisses it before returning his attention back to his father. I don't hear much of the rest of Warren's speech because my mind is busy intruding on my concentration.

Jared is serious about me. Taking me here, on his parent's thirty-fifth anniversary, is a monster-sized sign of that and I'm starting to like his family, too.

". . . please give a toast to my beautiful wife, Abby. Ever since our first kiss on Redondo Beach, under the stars that summer, I have never looked back. I love you."

Both sons are smiling and clapping at their parents as the guests watch them kiss.

Then the real party begins. Jason hired a live band and a DJ. With good music, great company and a never-ending supply of alcohol, everyone is having a blast, including me.

When the band starts to play *The Way You Look Tonight* in a slow jazzy beat, Jared gets up. "Dance with me?"

Smiling, I accept. "Sure"

Jared leads us to the dance floor, wraps his arms around me and pulls me close to his chest. The music draws me in as Jared takes over my senses. With his hot breath against my ear, our breathing accelerates as we dance to the slow beat. For a while, it makes me forget the kind of emotional turmoil that I'm in.

"Thank you for coming. My family adores you," Jared says after we've danced silently for a few moments.

"They're lovely. Thank you for inviting me and sharing this significant day."

His hand grips me tighter. "God, you smell great. Lil . . ." Jared's breathing shifts. "I want you."

I bite my lip as I contemplate what to say to him. "I know. Give me a few weeks, then I will be . . . ready for you. To be with you, I mean."

Shit, did I just say that? Two weeks to get over Drake? Was that even enough time?

"Is there another man? Is that why you're so hesitant?" Jared halts when the music stops.

Reaching for my hand, he guides me towards the other end of the garden, where there are no people around. The tall trees and rose bushes make it difficult to see, but Jared knows where he's going. He stops when we get to a fountain. The smell of roses are overpowering and toying with my senses. I have to concede that roses are definitely the smell of seduction.

I'm not panicking that I'm alone with Jared in the dark, but I'm a little hesitant to tell him about

Drake because if he starts shooting out questions, I may not have an answer for him. I can barely admit to most of the answers to myself . . . Never mind saying them out loud.

"Lily, I'm still waiting for you to answer my question." Jared is a couple of feet away from me. His hands are in his pockets, his face serious as he waits for me to speak.

Oh, fuck it. Jared deserves more than this. "A guy from my past recently came back into my life."

"An ex? Does he want you back? Where do I stand?" Jared looks devastated and I feel bad, actually, I feel like shit.

"No, not an ex, but he was my first. Things aren't really like that with us. I like you, Jared, very much." Jared pulls me up to my feet so we are facing each other.

"Alright, I understand where you are coming from, but the most important question is, do you want him back?"

Drake . . . I love him, but Shannon, their almost baby and the fucking past are always going to be there. When it comes down to it, I don't trust Drake not to break me again because he will. He already did once before, quite callously, too.

"No, I don't want him back," I state with conviction.

"Good. That's all I need to hear. Two weeks and you'll be mine?"

"Yes."

"Mine in two weeks, I can't wait until I can claim you as mine," Jared whispers before he takes my lips and kisses me.

The kiss is good, hungry even, but compared to Drake's . . . this kiss lacks something. Or maybe it's me who lacks something. Yeah, that would be my heart.

It's possible to lose your heart along the way. It dawns on me that life does go on after love. That one can go on with just a partial part of your heart—or none at all—depending on how much love you granted that person. In my case, I'm trying to scrape back what little I have left because Drake took most of it away, leaving me with the crumbs.

With that, though, I am determined to build something out of it. Maybe I'll grow another heart, another love.

16

Jared moves around the front of the car to open my door. Once I'm on the pavement, outside my townhouse, we stare at each other for a while, smiling.

"Thank you. I had a lot of fun tonight." I look at Jared before he claims my lips again.

This time, I let myself go and kiss him the way he's kissing me. Jared's hand lifts my skirt and cups my butt cheek, pushing it against his hardened state.

"Lily!" a voice barks out.

I open my eyes and find Drake fuming like a mad man ready to kill me and Jared—who happens to just let go of me. Something in Jared's eyes flares, but he composes himself. Both men measure each other up, readying for some testosterone showdown.

"Jared!" I pull him aside. "I'm sorry. Let me talk to him. I'll call you, okay?" I plead.

Jared's nose flares. "You want me to leave you with an angry man? Have you lost it? I don't trust him with you!"

No, this is not the time to be macho, damn it. "It's fine. He'll calm down. I just need to talk to him. Trust me on this one. Jared, please?"

Defeated, Jared cusses for a moment and then concedes. "Fine." He cups my cheek. "Call me, anytime, if something happens, okay?" He leans over and gives me another tongue lashing kiss.

"Thank you," I whisper to Jared before he gets in his car and drives off.

I stand on the pavement and watch until I can't see the lights of Jared's car. Then I turn around to deal with the ever present mistake, my problem.

"How dare you, Drake!" I screech at him.

His eyes are screaming bloody murder, but that doesn't scare me a bit. "How dare me? How dare you, Lily! You were barely out of my bed before you jump into another man's arms! How fucking dare YOU!" Drake spits back at me, glaring.

Right, slutty Lily. Yay, me!

"Goodnight, Drake." I stride past him and head for my door. With my key, I open it and I'm just about to take a step inside when Drake pushes me inside and slams me against the wall.

If it's possible for my heart to leap and do a marathon, my heart would be a champion at the rate it's going. "Go home, Drake."

"Stop killing me, Lil. What you did tonight . . . I wanted to commit fucking murder." He plants both hands against the wall on either side of my head when I try to move away from him. He's caging me in for confrontation. "Did you fuck him?" Drake barks.

"That's none of your business, Drake. I told you before that it wasn't. Now, I'm telling you again. I am not yours. Never was."

"You were last night when you kept screaming my name as you came. I think I'm half deaf from your screams alone."

Bring that up, why don't you? "That was last night, big difference."

Drake growls. "Why do you toy with me and my emotions? Is this some kind of punishment because of what happened eight years ago? I'm sorry. Okay, I fucked up, but it's different now. I fucking want you."

No matter how hard I try not to be affected by his words, they still manage to get through and cut deep inside me. I'm speechless for a moment before I can respond. "You're eight years too late, Drake." I finally manage to squeak out.

The pounding of my heart is deafening. Drake's heavy breathing is distracting and it doesn't help that he's so close. Nor does it help that my body's acting all weird again. Betraying me.

It itches to be touched by him; to be marked by him.

Drake's eyes are determined. He's not going to let this go. "I don't—I choose not to believe you. I won't. It's crazy, Lil, but my gut tells me that you're lying. Your mouth speaks of hate, but your body says something else. So, which one should I believe and trust?" His thumb reaches out and traces the side of my neck, stroking.

It stops at my pulse and I stiffen. "I didn't realize that you're such a liar now, Lily. I did tell you that your body doesn't lie to me."

"Stop it." I gasp when his hand moves lower. My chest is heaving like I've ran for miles. I'm out of breath from anticipation, anger, frustration, and, yes . . . excitement.

FUCK!

I squeezed my eyes shut when his middle finger reaches inside my corset, and brushes against my pebbled nipple. "Yes, you are a liar," Drake states confidently. "Or is your body wrong, Babe?"

Yes, it's wrong. I shouldn't want you, but I do. So, fucking, bad. It's not right, to want you this much. I must be fucked up beyond belief to want you this badly.

"Yes, it's wrong. You're wrong," I speak, panting and out of breath.

"Huh."

"Drake!" I yell when his hand goes up under my skirt. His hand is purposeful as it nudges the side of my underwear and then sticks a finger inside me.

Fucking, asshole, I hate you.

"Your pussy doesn't think so," Drake pants against my ear. I moan when he starts to stroke me tenaciously before he jabs another finger into me.

My God, I'm dying. "Don't do this . . ." I whisper, but my body is betraying me. It screams for more; more of Drake and more of this erotic torture.

"I'm not stopping until you tell me the truth, but if you want to play stubborn, this can go on all night. I won't mind it at all."

"What truth? Argh, shit, Drake!" I clutch onto his shoulders, practically hyperventilating from his fingers. "Drake . . ." I cry out.

I hear him growl when he rips another pair of my thongs. The second one in twenty-four hours. With my thong out of the way, things get more serious. "I'm not going to let you come, unless you give in to me."

Cruel son of a bitch! "Fuck you!" I curse at him, at my stupid body, at every single thing because when his fingers almost withdraw, I grind my hips against them, begging for more. "Ahh, ahh . . ." I moan.

"Do you want me?" Drake fumbles with something. I hear his pants drop on the floor next.

"Ahumm . . ." I say incoherently.

"What? I can't hear you. I'm asking again, do you want me to fuck you?"

"No . . ."

Drake hoists me up against the wall and rams his hard cock inside me, with one hard thrust. "Oh, God, It's so tight. This tight cunt is mine," he repeats each time he slides back inside me. "I own this cunt. Tell me I'm the owner."

"Hell, no!"

Drake curses and hoists me up again, carrying me towards my living room. With his manhood still inside me, he cups my chin and kisses me senseless.

Was this his way of making me submit to him? Using my body against me? It's working effectively.

Done fighting with my body, I kiss him back, angered and impassioned. *Just for tonight . . .* I think as I start to rock my hips against his cock. Drake makes a guttural sound. Holding onto my hips, he uses them to make my body pound against him, roughly, ruthlessly. He fucks me hard and kisses me harder. I hang on to him, kissing him as I run my nails down his back.

I stop kissing him when I realize we aren't using condoms again. Fuck! "Protection. Condom, Drake."

"No. Not with you, never with you. We'll get you pills tomorrow." He quickly places me on all fours on the chaise lounge. He then parts my legs, presses his hand on my lower back to keep me in the position he wants me in and enters me, viciously.

My knees buckle as pleasure, pain and soreness hits me full-on. In this position, he has easy access to the deepest parts of me. I'm not sure if I can handle it. If he pounds me any harder, I might not recover. "Drake . . . I . . . um..."

"Does it hurt?" he distractedly asks while his other hand reaches over my stomach, parts my folds and lets his fingers cater to my core. "Babe?" Drake asks as he starts to gradually move. Hissing each time he slides back into me.

Heck, yes, it hurts like a bitch, but I don't want him to stop, either. "Don't stop. Just keep going."

"Come here, Babe." Drake slowly pulls me against his chest, takes my chin and kisses me. On our knees with his cock buried deep inside my core and his fingers on my clit, he passionately devours my lips. My body starts to relax while I press my back against his chest. When his cock starts to move inside me, the soreness is still there, but the pleasure is terrifyingly amazing; it's all I can concentrate on.

Drake's pacing starts to heighten again, but this time, I am ready to take him in. "Get on your elbows, lower your upper body, but lift your ass to me."

"Argh! Fuck!" I cry out when he severely smacks my ass a few times.

"No more other men, Lil. I won't be accountable for what happens next time I see you going on dates or another man touching you. Are we clear?"

Damn it. "I don't think you and I will work out, Drake. This is just sex."

He smacks my ass again and thrusts forward, teasing me. "How the heck do you figure that? We haven't even tried it."

We haven't really tried, but . . . what else do I have to lose? I already lost my heart to him. Can I possibly make him love me the way I love him? I'm still pondering it when Drake suddenly pulls out of me.

He stands up, takes his shirt off and throws it away. He then goes over and punches a wall.

What the hell? I watch him fume. Meanwhile, I drop off the couch and sit on the carpet, admiring his naked form. God, his ass is to die for.

Seriously, I have it bad. Really, fucking, bad.

Drake runs his hands through his hair as he mutters something. "Fuck!" he yells at the wall. After huffing a few more times, he finally spins around and stalks towards me.

I train my eyes very hard to not look down and away from him; no matter how much I really want to look away, I can't. I won't give him an inch on this. Drake kneels down next to me, looking helpless and agonized. "Tell me what to do. I'll do it," he rasps out, voice packed with emotion.

"Drake—"

He cuts me off. "Just tell me. Do you want me to grovel? Do you want me on my knees and asking for forgiveness? Just say it, Lil, so I can jump through anything you ask of me. I'll do anything to have you, be with you, and have you beside me."

Just love me. It's all I have ever wanted.

"Are you sure you're not on the rebound after Shannon?" I eye him warily. Drake's asking me to put my heart on the line for him, again. I have to know what's on the table and what isn't.

"Un-fucking-believable!" He gets up again, nose flaring, furious. He paces and stops, looking down at me. "Use your fucking head, will you? Do you think I will fuck around with a woman, whom my parents wish to be my wife? Have you not seen the changes in me, Lily? The moment I saw you again, there was no doubt in my mind that I wanted you. I always have, but this time, I'm ready to give you my all."

That does it! He's ready. Great! Yippee! "Before, you didn't want me because you weren't ready? Now, that you've grown, you're ready for me? How fucking convenient, Drake." I get up, angry, with shaky legs. It doesn't deter me. "I loved you. I fucking loved you! I worshipped the ground you walked on. And you knew it, too! Even before I told you, you knew how I felt about you." I swallow, my throat constricting, as my tears threaten to fall. "But you didn't care. You just took what you wanted and walked away. For eight fucking years, never once have I heard from you. Not. Once."

I start to shiver, but I'm not done. "How do you expect me to react to you, now that you want me the way I wanted you to want me eight years ago? Did you expect me to jump for joy because you've changed your mind about me? Newsflash, the world doesn't revolve around you and your wishes. You can go fuck yourself!" I start to walk out of the living room, wiping my tears away, when his words stop me.

"I went to visit you once. That same year. It was Christmas Eve, but you were wrapped up with some guy. I was actually a few feet away. I was even surprised that you didn't notice me. Guess you were too busy with him.

"You see, I wanted to talk to you. About what happened that summer and how for six months on, I still couldn't get you out of my head. You looked happy, Lil. I thought it was for the best. I thought, when you told me you loved me then, it was just a crush. You were young. I mean, what did you know about love when you were eighteen, right? So, I did what I thought was best and left you alone."

"What guy?" I whisper, still halted on the same spot. There had been no one, no one for two years after him. The only guy I hung out with was Nick, Masie's boyfriend, who became a friend, too.

"Tall, dark hair and fairly built. I didn't stay long enough to watch you with him. I couldn't stand it."

"Nick. The guy you saw me with was Nick. He's my friend's boyfriend who is a very good friend of mine." Drake went to see me. Sadness fills me in an instant. Missed opportunity . . . if it hadn't gone that way . . . maybe I wouldn't have a grudge against him. Even if he and I end up not pursuing a relationship together, at least I have some sort of closure now and not some twisted, pathetic reasoning my brain can juggle with.

A person cannot fully and truly understand the meaning of bitterness, gripping pain and raw heartache if one hasn't gone through a massive blow of rejection—the kind, where it demolishes all your confidence and self-worth. The kind, where life halts and your heart is left in that suspended time, with him, reliving memories; the good and the bad, over and over again.

I lived. I breathed. I simply existed.

That's all I was, all I've ever been, since Drake crushingly and devastatingly left me. There is nothing worse than being brushed off by someone you love so much and hold dearly, it leaves you feeling as if you're worth nothing. I've been a shell, an empty shell, because of this man. It's sad, that the moment I am back in his arms again, I feel whole, complete. How can I fathom such a trivial pursuit of happiness? Am I even capable of risking whatever that is left of me to be with Drake again?

"I'm sorry" he croaks out, gutted.

I hear him move, cautiously. Paralyzed, I hold my breath as I feel his hard chest against my back, his hot breath hitting my left shoulder. "I'll do what you ask of me. Just tell me what to do. One more chance is all I ask. I know this might be too much to ask of you, but if you feel the same as I do, I want you to reconsider."

"Okay," I rasp out, my voice trembling.

"Okay, yes? I want to be with you, too? Or is it an okay, I will think about it, kind of okay?" Drake asked cautiously.

I spin around, facing his naked form. I look up at his nervous face and I can't quite look him in the eyes, my eyes drop low, looking at his chest. With my right hand, I softly press against his beating heart. "I want to be with you, but . . . you have to understand, that it may take longer for me to trust you. You have to earn it. This is not easy . . . for me to do. I know one thing that's true and that is how much I still feel about you." Choked up, I meet Drake's gaze. "Let's take this one day at a time. Is that alright with you?"

A smile starts to break across his handsome face. "You're really serious? You won't change your mind tomorrow? Because if that's the case, I don't think I can handle it."

"Well, maybe you should try and not make me change my mind, then. It certainly wouldn't hurt for you to try and be irresistible for once," I goad him.

He mildly chortles and wraps his arms around me. "You're definitely sure, Babe?" Drake presses on, needing assurance.

"I am. Happy now?"

"You bet I am." We are both laughing as our lips touch. Once our kiss deepens, our laughter dies.

Drake hungrily growls as he hoists me up. Automatically, my legs wrap around his hips. I'm out of breath almost instantly and ready to finish what we started earlier.

"Bed? Where's your bed?" Drake asks in between kisses.

"Upstairs, on the right."

Drake hurriedly takes us upstairs while we continue making out. When we accidentally bump the railing, I bust out laughing. "Calm down; you're going to get us killed."

"That should tell you how crazy I am about you." Drake smacks my ass before he grips both cheeks and grinds my mound against his raging hard-on.

In my bedroom, we both land on the bed. Drake's hands work double time on ripping my clothes off. Once I'm naked, he crawls over my body, eyes drinking me in. "Thank you," he softly speaks.

Those two words profoundly affect me. I suppose he knows how difficult it is for me to take a chance on him again.

Drake slowly and softly starts to kiss my neck. "It's my turn to worship you. I do worship the ground that you walk on, Lil. It wasn't just you, Babe."

Would it be too cheesy if I simply swell with love for him?

Drake shows me just how much he worships me, a few times, with his tongue and fingers alone. The rest, I simply lose count. We ride each other into oblivion.

17

I wake up with Drake's arm latched on to me so tight that it's impossible to move.

"Drake, I need to move." I nudge his arm to wake him up.

He whiningly groans as his mouth searches out the back of my neck, giving it a few kisses. "I love waking up next to you, too."

"It's already past noon. We have to get up." Still, he holds me tight, fingers stroking the side of my leg.

"But I want to stay in bed all day with—" He pauses, suddenly jolts and sits up. "Fuck! I forgot about Skull!"

Finally, I'm able to roll over to my other side and touch his back, stroking it. "What about Skull? Is there something wrong with him?"

Drake shakes his head. "No, but he doesn't like to be on his own in the house. That's why he stays with Mom and Dad if I'm not home." Sighing, he scrambles to his feet.

I sit up. "Wait—where are you going?" I'm baffled by his immediate withdrawal.

"Skull gets lonely. He's probably been crying all night."

Amused, I bite my lip, smiling. "Hold on. Let me get this straight. You're rushing to get home because your dog is lonely?"

Drake stands, watching my lit up face, hands on his hips, bold in all his naked glory. "Are you making fun of me?"

"Maybe, it's just that, never in a million years have I pictured you being like this, all because of a dog. It's really hot."

"Oh, yeah?" He leans over and gives me a chaste kiss on the lips. "Come with me, please? I want to spend more time with you and frankly, I'm not ready to be away from you yet."

Like I would let him leave all on his own, especially after last night . . .

"Give me ten minutes to shower and get ready." I slide off the bed. Not shy about my naked body in broad daylight.

Standing close to each other, Drake kisses my forehead. "Just put some clothes on. We can shower at my place."

"Fine, as long as you promise to make me lunch." I love it when he's all sweet. He makes me feel beautiful just being this way.

"Deal. Now get a move on," he says before he playfully smacking my ass loudly, shooing me away to change.

======

I stare at the dog, then at the owner, and then back at the dog again before I start shrieking with laughter.

I stop when Skull starts barking at me for causing such a loud commotion. Wiping my tears away, I manage to look at Drake without laughing, but my eyes dance anyways. "When you mentioned your dog's name was Skull, I was imagining a pug or a bulldog. Something manly, you know? I'm . . . I'm just shocked to find that Skull is a puffy brown and white Pomeranian."

Drake comes over and picks up his doggy, holding Skull against his chest before the dog gives him a few wet licks on the lips. "Show her that you're made of hard stuff, Baby," he coos.

I smirk. Drake really does love this dog of his.

He puts him back down on the floor before he wraps his arms around me, smelling my neck. "Now, what would you like for lunch?"

We spend the rest of our Saturday in his house. Kissing, talking and catching up. By the end of the day, I've bonded with Skull and I think he favors me more than Drake.

It's most likely because I sneak him a treat or two when Drake isn't watching.

=====

A painful scream comes out of me when I feel someone jerk my hair and arm, dragging me off the bed and onto the floor.

"You, stupid whore. Didn't I warn you to stay away from him? I did, didn't I? But you didn't fucking listen! He's mine!" Shannon shrieks at me.

Since I'm on the floor, the closest thing I can reach is her leg. I pull it hard enough for her to lose her balance and she flops onto the floor next to me with a loud thud.

Shannon is scrambling to get on top of me when Drake yanks her off, throwing her off where she lands on the bed.

She is hysterically crying. "How dare you bring her here! On our bed! This was our bed. How fucking dare you, Drake! You're mine. You're mine . . ."

"You and I are done, Shannon. I've made that clear already. I have your key. How the fuck did you get in here?" Drake is glaring at her, eyes dark, furious.

My heart is sky-rocketing, beating so hard against my chest; it's the only thing I feel. That is, until I start to feel the pain on my head. The spot where Shannon pulled my hair is beginning to throb and ache.

"Stupid man, do you think I would hand it over without having it copied? It's not like you changed your security code, anyway. It was easy. You're saying that we're over when she's around, but I know you still want me. You always have. We're about to get married, Drake. You can't keep hurting me like this." Shannon starts crying again. She tries to reach out to Drake, but he smacks her hand away.

Drake helps me up and carefully places me on one of the cushioned chairs that are on the other side of the room. "Are you okay? Fuck, I'm sorry. Are you hurting?"

"I'm fine. Go take care of that, first." My eyes send daggers to his deranged ex. Who is still in the process of crying and pleading.

Hell, what the heck did I get myself into?

Drake grabs his cellphone and dials the cops. He reports a home invasion and illegal trespassing. As he rapidly speaks on the phone, it's hard to follow.

I feel numb.

My body is still tense and I'm afraid to move for some reason—possibly because the senseless bitch is still on the bed—sending me crazy eyes when Drake isn't watching her.

When the cops come, Drake takes the reluctant Shannon downstairs. I hear him ask them to take her to the hospital first to get checked over. Just in case she's high on something.

I feel something wet on my leg and when I look down, I find Skull rubbing his nose on me. I bend down and scratch the back of his ears. He then curls up next to my foot and falls asleep. The adorable fur ball is giving me comfort.

After what seems to be an hour of answering all the questions the police have for Drake, he finally comes back upstairs with some Advil and an icepack.

He finds me, sitting, still in the same position I was in when he left with Shannon. "Are you okay? You don't look well."

I nod and swallow the pills with some water. Drake carefully takes me in his arms and carries me into one of the guest rooms. We lie on the bed with Skull leaning on my back, snoring. I'm wrapped around Drake's body while he holds the icepack to my head.

Drake breaks the silence first. "I didn't think she was crazy. Okay, I mean towards the end, she started to become off, but I didn't think for a second she was capable of pulling something like that. I'm just thankful that she didn't have a knife . . . or a gun. God knows what would've happened if she did."

I would probably be dead by now, or I would've killed that daft bitch first. Hell, her crazy eyes are still haunting me. I remember the hate and scorn in those eyes and I shiver.

When the painkillers work their way into my system, Drake takes the icepack off my head.

He's stroking my arm, softly, as I finally drift off to sleep.

18

"I have to go home and get ready for your mom's lunch party."

We just finished eating breakfast where I nibbled on a toast and had some coffee. Honestly, the last thing I want to do is eat or go to a lunch party after last night, but I promised my mom. Today is important to her and I can't let her down.

"How about you let me shower quickly, then we can drive back to your house and go to my parents' house together?" Drake asks before taking a swig of his coffee.

"About that . . . I don't want them to get any ideas, yet. I want to keep this between you and me for a while, if you don't mind?"

"I do mind. Why would you want to keep me as your dirty, little secret?" Drake nods, the answer just dawning on him. "Right, in case this doesn't work out between us," he says through gritted teeth.

"Don't get angry. I just don't want all the fuss. We barely just started. I want to keep it that way for now. I did tell you that we'll be taking it one step at a time."

Drake merely shrugs, and then looks away, hurt.

=====

Drake's car is already parked in his parents' driveway when I get there. As I'm pulling into an open space in the drive, my ringing phone distracts me from thoughts of Drake.

"Hey, Masie! What's up?"

"You're still coming for the barbeque this afternoon, right? Just checkin', that's all." Masie's chirpy demeanor helps ease my tensed body.

"Yep, I did say I was coming. Gotta go, Hon, I'm going to meet Mom's boyfriend for the first time." Hopefully, everything will be okay.

"Okay, see you in a few."

After ending the call with Masie, I sit in the car, killing time. I took a couple of painkillers before I left my house, but it seems that it's taking forever to kick-in. My head throbs and my arm hurts like it's strained.

I lean back against the seat, closing my eyes, rubbing the area on my arm that is aching. *Maybe, I have to get something stronger to dull the pain away,* I think.

"Lily?" I hear Drake knock on my window. Without opening my eyes, I unlock my door and open it.

"Give me a minute. I should be out soon," I mumble in response.

"Are you hurting, Babe?" Drake looks worried as he squats down to my level and checks my arm.

I flinch when he touches the sore spot. "Just a little, but I already took some pain meds before I left the house. I'm still waiting for it to kick in."

Drake takes off my seatbelt and gathers me in his arms. "I'm taking you in. You need to rest."

"I can walk. Put me down," I protest. "Drake, I will rest, okay? But you have to let me walk. I can't imagine what they will think if you burst inside the house with me hanging in your arms."

Drake sighs. "I was only thinking about your welfare, Lil."

I give him a quick kiss, which helps his mood. "I know." I smile at him.

We slowly walk towards the entrance. Drake drops his arm off my shoulder once we enter the foyer. The Tatum's Spanish-style residence is majestic. It has twelve bedrooms, a crazy amount of bathrooms, two kitchens, two pools and a huge tennis court.

=====

"Lily, I'm so happy you could make it." Patricia kisses my cheek and gives me a warm hug before she lets go and kisses my forehead.

"Drake's not being a pain is he, Hon? If he is, you go straight to me." Patricia eyes us with a huge smile.

"Mom, Lily doesn't feel too well. I'm about to take her upstairs and let her rest for a bit." Drake stands a little closer to me.

"Of course, go say hi to your mom first, so she doesn't worry. Do you need any medicine?" She doesn't even let me respond to that before she orders Drake to tell someone in the kitchen to prepare some food for me and he can take it upstairs with him.

"I already plan on it, Mom," Drake murmurs before walking away.

"Your mother is in the dining room with Colin and Hugh." Patricia pauses. "You're okay with her dating again, right? Your mom is happy. I can vouch for that." You can see she is worried that I won't approve of Mom's new love life; it's written all over her face.

"I am, Pat. I'm glad she did. She needs someone to be there for her, too. I'm actually pleased that it's with Colin. At least we know the man already."

Patricia looks radiant. "That is true. It's just been too long for her. She deserves it." Pat clears her throat and eyes me. "I don't mean to pry... but I can't help it. Drake can't take his eyes off you. Please tell me that he's trying to win you? You know there's nothing in this world that would please me more... Drake and you together. It's my only wish." She looks expectant as she waits for me to speak.

Yes, Patricia. We all know it. I want to say that Drake and I are actually together, but I don't want to get her hopes up. "All I can tell you is . . . I guess, he's trying."

She is overjoyed. "That man . . . I keep telling him that there will be no other woman who will make him as happy as you, Lil. Every time I tell him that, he tells me to drop the subject, but I guess, it did get through to him. The way my son looks at you, he won't stop until he gets what he wants."

"I know," I whisper. I remember how relentless he can be and I clearly remember how he has been since I've succumbed to him. He's insatiable and I love every second of it. The man knows his way around a woman's body. I blush as I recall his antics.

Patricia and I go into the dining room and join the rest of the group. I greet Mom, Hugh and Colin. Colin is still pleasant and still looks the same since I last saw him. Which was ages ago. Patricia explains that I'm not feeling too well, but before I leave the dining room, I see her wickedly wink at me.

I meander back towards the hall and find Drake waiting for me at the stairs, leaning against the staircase. My body prickles when I get close to him. "Hi."

"Ready?" Drake asks.

I frown. "For what?"

Drake picks me up and takes me upstairs to his old bedroom. How he manages to get there without tripping, I will never know. Once we are next to his bed, he slowly puts me down and undresses me until I only have my bra and underwear on. He then puts me in his bed and covers me with the sheets.

"You might not be hungry, but I'm going to feed you anyway," Drake says as he takes a tray of food and places it on the side table. The smell of fresh sautéed shrimps, grilled steak and vegetables makes my mouth water. "Open your pretty little mouth, Lil."

I glare at him. "I can feed myself."

He shakes his head. "Nope, where's the fun in that? Let me take care of you, Babe."

Damn the man for being so sweet. I can't help but say 'yes' every single time this side of him comes out.

So he feeds me until I'm full. Drake wants me to finish the entire raspberry topped crème brûlée, but I'm way past my limit. "I can't . . . no more. You've already proved to be such a good nurse. I'm good." I grin at him.

Drake stands up and puts the tray aside after he carefully cleans my lips of any food residue. "What now?" I look at him, expectantly.

"What do you want to do? Do you want to rest? I can get you more pain meds if you need them." Drake sits on the bed and starts to stroke his fingers against mine.

Emboldened, I tell him, "I want your kisses. Can you make that happen?"

Drake jumps right on the bed and gets on top of me. "Thought you'd never ask," he murmurs before he kisses me with such affection, I hopelessly burn against him.

I run my fingers through his hair, playfully pulling it. Drake groans against my lips. "Relax and sit tight while my mouth devours you."

I yelp when Drake situates his head in between my core and bites into the flesh of my inner thigh. "You're too playful," I complain. I hear his light chuckle and feel his hot breath against my mound as he removes my panties.

"You have no idea . . . how playful I can be." My fingers clutch the sheets when his tongue pierces into my wet entrance. Those were the last words he spoke to me for an hour and half.

19

"Masie, this is Drake. He wanted to tag along. I hope you don't mind me bringing him without giving you a heads up." I look at my smiling, curious friend.

She might be smiling, but I know what she might be truly thinking behind the façade. She's probably freaking out and jumping for joy that I brought Drake here.

"Ah, I've heard a lot about you, Drake. Nice to finally meet you. When Lily said you were good-looking, I didn't realize she was lying. 'Cause you're more than good looking." Masie greets him and Drake blushes from Masie's boldness.

"You asked for it. You did invite yourself to come along," I mutter next to him.

"Nice to meet you, Masie." Drake hands her a bottle of red wine before Masie leads us inside.

Masie doesn't hold back when she checks Drake's backside as he moves past her, then gives me a thumbs-up. I simply glare at her. "It's just us and a few of our close friends." Masie informs Drake.

I stop when I see Jared outside, laughing and drinking a beer.

Hell, am I being punished? Why are bad things happening to me? When it rains, it pours, they say. Now I know what that phrase truly means.

When Drake sees my expression, he follows to where my gaze has landed. He immediately tenses behind me. "Try to behave will you, Lil?" Drake asks me in a low tone, just loud enough for me to hear.

"Scared that I'll ditch you for another man?" I'm beyond amused. Drake is really possessive. He cusses and I just give him a bright smile.

"Don't worry, you can't be easily replaced."

Drake starts to thaw, just a tad. "You mean that, Lil?"

Always, Drake. "Yes, I do mean it."

When we go out to the backyard and join the rest of the party. Jared smiles when he sees me, but that smile turns into a frown once he spies Drake, who follows behind me.

Masie introduces Drake to the rest of her friends. Nick eyes Drake before he shakes hands with him. I'm guessing Nick instantly knows who he is, based on his reaction. "Welcome, Drake." Nick motions for Drake to take a seat and join them at the table. There are a dozen or so of their friends sitting around the table.

As the party goes on, Nick, David and Drake are engrossed in their talk about movies and special effects. I decide to go inside and help Masie out in the kitchen instead of trying to follow the guys' conversation. I hardly notice when Jared follows me in.

"Lily, can we talk?"

I clear my throat before I agree. Jared leads us to the living room for some privacy. Jared chooses to stand towards the very end of the room, away from where I am.

"The weeks you promised, I guess that's not valid any longer?" he asks accusingly.

"The other night, we sorted things out somehow. I want to give Drake another chance. I have to. I feel that I owe it to myself to know if it could really work or not. I meant to tell you," I plead to Jared. He looks like he can't believe what I'm telling him.

"I really like you, Lily. You must know that. I'm hurt, yeah. Although, I'm not going to lie and say I didn't see this one coming after leaving you the other night with him being so angry." Jared sits on the beige couch and huffs out a sigh. "Tell the guys that I'm going home. I need to clear my head for the day. I just got hit by a big blow. I need time to process this, if you don't mind." He suddenly stands up and walks towards where I stand, rooted on the spot.

I feel like the most wretched person for making this sweet guy miserable. There is no other way to go about it. I want Drake and I want to see where this can go. I'm done denying what my heart's been telling me since the day that he came back into my life.

Jared kisses my cheek. "I knew that this man owned your heart when I saw how you reacted to him. Follow where your heart leads you . . . and be happy. Take care, Lil."

"Thank you, Jared," I say with gratitude for his understanding.

He gives me a sad, shaky smile before leaving the living room and out of the house.

After a few minutes, Masie comes in and gathers me in her arms. "Don't feel too bad, Missy. I think we all know that your heart lies with Drake after all these years. Jared knew the score. Nick tried to warn him off, but he didn't listen."

Masie and I join the rest of party. When one of the guys asks where Jared went, she just shrugs, tells them that he had to sort something out and needed to leave immediately.

"Everything okay, Babe?" Drake whispers against my ear when I sit next to him. He sounds worried. I'm grateful that he didn't freak out when Jared followed me inside. Knowing how Drake is, he most likely saw it, but trusted me to take care of it and I did; I took care of it.

I brightly smile at him before I give him a quick kiss. "It is now."

His pauses and looks me over. "Yeah?"

"Yeah, Drake."

His pleased, beautiful smile does me in. "Thank you. That makes me so happy. I'll show you how happy I am tonight." Drake's eyes burn me up. I feel my cheeks grow hot and my vaginal muscles tighten.

Damn the man. He's getting me aroused right in front of my friends.

His shrewd eyes figure out what is going on with my body as he sees the changes in me. His eyes dilate as he stares at me. I'm surprised when he suddenly stands up and excuses us both. "I have to speak to Lily for a bit. Please excuse us."

Since they are busy talking about playing poker, they don't mind us leaving.

Drake quickly leads us upstairs and shoves me inside the bathroom where he locks us in. "I need to be inside you. Now!" He hisses against my ear as he positions me facing the mirror, against the sink. His hands take care of my jeans along with my underwear, pulling them down just past my knees.

"Are you wet?" Drake urgently asks as his finger checks. "You are . . . dripping . . ." He groans against my neck. I hear his pants fall on the floor before he speaks again. "Bend over. Don't part your legs. I want to take you like this. I know you're tight as it is, but I want to feel you break open while I stretch you further. Hold tight because I'm not going to take you fast this time."

My eyes stay glued to the mirror as his hips thrust forward, the head of his cock parting my folds. "Do you feel the difference when you don't part your legs? My dick can barely fit in there."

I'm panting so hard, I can barely think. Though he has a hard time sliding it in all the way in, he is persistent. He pulls out and puts it back in, inching deeper inside me with each thrust. It teases my hunger, sucking me into a sexual cloud that I can't get enough of. The more he teases, the hungrier I become.

"Do it, just fucking do it," I dare him to just hit it all the way home. I anticipate the pain it will bring, but I know that Drake will make up for it.

Drake grabs both of my ass cheeks while he bites my earlobe as he rams his cock into me hard until it hits the wall of my cervix. I grunt from the painful throb. "Keep your ass up as I instructed you earlier. Don't you dare move. My cock's going to love you until you can't take it anymore. Is that what you want, Babe?" The head of his shaft teases the wall of my womb.

"You're all talk," I moan against him.

"Remember, you asked for this," Drake informs me before he pulls out and drives in with precision.

I'm shaking and sobbing his name in a minute as I come, my muscles contracting against his moving shaft. My hand pushes against the mirror as he annihilates my body, taking me to the next level. "Don't move!" Drake hisses against my shoulder.

"I can't . . . too much." Tears prickle in my eyes as my body starts to tighten again, readying for another wave of release.

"Let go," Drake commands as my body does just that, but he isn't finished. Not by a long shot.

My body is trembling more than I thought possible. My strength to keep the position he ordered is thinning. "One more?" he asks as he slows down, his dick still stroking me while his lips rain kisses on the back of my neck. "Tilt your head a bit. I want your lips."

Our lips touch, passion licks my soul as our tongues fight, fervently. Drake powers into my depths with titillating force as he impales me with his hard shaft. Striking me deeper, taking me to another dimension. His hands press against my stomach as he pierces me with his throbbing cock. "Come for me, Babe," Drake instructs again before he bites into my shoulder. It makes me convulse around him. I cry out as an orgasm takes hold of my body.

Drake rolls his hips a few more times before he hisses out a few angry curses. He comes beautifully as I watch him in the mirror. He is incredible to watch. My eyes find his in the mirror, his cock still pulsating inside me. "You love watching me go crazy, I see." Drake smiles as he kisses my neck.

"I can't help it. You look too hot to resist." Hopeless, that's me, alright.

Drake pulls out and spins me around, kissing me hard. "You're amazing. Do you know that? I'm so crazy about you."

"I'm crazy about you, too."

"Good to know that the feeling is mutual. Let's go join your friends, and then we can head home. I want you alone." Drake kisses me one more time before he cleans me off with a wet paper towel.

=====

We've just finished our shower together and are in bed, ready to sleep, when Drake speaks into the dark.

"Lil?"

I perk up. "Hmmm?"

"I was thinking; why don't you start working on your business plan with Masie? I can hire another person. You guys were pretty excited discussing the possibility of it earlier, so why not do it? Go look for a place tomorrow to rent. Go over business details and open up in the next three months?"

"Is this your subtle way of firing me? Will you be hiring a hot blonde as my replacement?"

"No. If it will make you happy, I will hire an efficient gay man. I had one before named Kip, but Shannon fired him when I was out of the country. I could contact him again and offer an incentive, but my point is, I want you to work on something that you love to do. It's time, Lil."

I know it's time for me to really go out there and do my thing.

I kiss his chest and whisper against it. "I know, thank you for bringing it up. I'll speak to Masie first thing in the morning." My hand touches his neck where it begins to curve to his shoulder.

"Good. I think this will be a good step for you," Drake murmurs against my forehead before he drifts off to sleep.

20

For the next two weeks, Masie and I are busy with our plans. We've been baking non-stop in my kitchen as we try different recipes; marking which ones work and which ones don't.

It's already six in the evening before Masie decides it's time to leave. We've been up since nine and only took half an hour lunch break before we started baking again.

"Are you sure you're going to be okay? You look nervous all of a sudden." Masie's instincts are spot on, but I'm not about to spill my secret. Not yet, anyway.

I merely nod. "Just tired. The last two weeks have been draining me." They have and now I have another issue to top it all off.

Masie gives me a cheerful smile. "Okay. Tell lover boy not to wear you out so much. You look like you need sleep." She winks at me before she leaves the house.

That, too. Drake has been insatiable on a daily basis. It's hard to keep up with him.

I'm sitting on the couch when I hear him enter the house. I left the door unlocked knowing he'd be over soon. "Hi."

Drake strolls in wearing an all-black Armani suit, looking like sex on legs. He bends over and kisses me on the lips. "How was your day, Pretty One?"

I look Drake dead in the eye and blurt it out, "I'm pregnant."

Drake suddenly stills before he composes himself. He opens his mouth, then shuts it again before he starts to pace around my living room. Calmly, he asks, "Is it mine?"

I feel like he just punched me in the gut while slapping me a few times before he stomps and spits on me. How dare he ask me that question? "On second thought, let me double check my calendar. It might not be yours after all."

I didn't anticipate him asking if it was his. I feel side-tracked and insulted. So, this was how Shannon must've felt.

Drake simmers in anger, but he asked for it. His question was beyond disrespectful.

"Please, leave. You are not welcome here anymore." I'm surprised that my voice is stern and it doesn't waver. I'm a wreck inside, but I'd rather die than show him that.

"Is it mine or not? Don't be a smartass about it. Answer the question as I asked you to do." His voice grates on me.

"Not yours, Drake."

He doesn't even dare look at me as he leaves my house, slamming the door shut on his way out.

It hurt that he would even question me like that. I told him I hadn't slept with anyone but him in over a year.

He can go suck on it for all I care. I don't need him to raise a child. I can take care of it on my own.

I don't need him.
I don't.

=====

I wake up the next day with a surprise. My mother is in my kitchen making me breakfast.

"Mom? What are you doing here so early? It's not even nine in the morning." I yawn while I sit down at the breakfast nook.

"Drake came by today. He told me that you're pregnant. Is that true?" Mom's eagle-eyes don't miss a beat. "And looking at your reaction, I'm assuming that it is Drake's, too?"

Fuck you, Drake Tatum, and your stupid tattle mouth. "He doesn't want it."

"He tells me that you told him he isn't the father." Mom places the food on the table before she slides it across to me, eyeing me sternly. "What made you say that, if he is the father?"

"The stupid man asked me if it was his. How dare he? I'm not some slut who's been juggling different guys. That was uncalled for." Okay, I need to calm down before I blow a fuse.

"Okay, maybe he did deserve that. From what I saw earlier, I can tell you that he's regretful, but doesn't know how to approach you."

"He can go fuck himself," I mutter.

"Lily, behave."

"I'm sorry, Mom, but I'm not in the mood to talk about this right now."

"You are an adult, Dear; we have to talk about this. Patricia will want to know and frankly, Drake is waiting for my call. The man didn't sleep a wink last night. He told me that's he's ready to marry you as well."

Fucking Drake.

"I am not marrying anyone. Period. As far as I am concerned, Drake and I are done. He can help out with the baby later on, but that's it."

"That's up to you, but you have to talk it out with Drake. He needs to hear it from you." My mom is always so reasonable. I know she wants what is best for me and Drake, but right now, I could care less. Drake royally pissed me off last night and that's that. True, he can be sorry, but that won't take back the words he spoke.

He fucked up, big time.

Mom gets up and hugs me. "I love you. You're going to be a great mom. Don't let hatred consume you, though. I think it's high time you and Drake sort this out." She kisses my forehead before walking towards the end of the room.

I hear her talking on the phone. I can't really blame her since this is such a big deal to us. We are a close unit. She and Pat are expecting their first grandchild and both have been dying for one.

"We're going over to the Tatum's for lunch. Will that be good for you?" Mom asks kindly.

It's not like I have a choice. If I don't agree to it, I full well know that the entire Tatum clan will be on my doorstep before sun down. "Yeah, sounds good to me."

21

"Lily doesn't want me. Her lying about my child proves that," Drake grates out as both of our mothers just look speechless.

"What do you want, Lily?" Patricia looks at me kindly.

What do I want? That's a good question to ask. I do want Drake, but not like this. It feels wrong. I don't want to be the next Shannon, robbing him of his life and livelihood. I am not that woman. Even if every fiber in me is screaming to just drop it and be with him.

"The baby and I are going to be okay. I mean, I have all of you guys to help out, right? Let's just take this one day at a time. Everything seems to be all new to me. So, please, calm down." I give Mom and Patricia a forced smile. Both women get up and hug me, telling me how much they love me.

"Thank you, Lil! Not only did you grant your mother's wishes to have a child, but mine as well. If you and Drake don't ever get married, though, I think you two should, as the mother of my unborn grandchild, you are my unofficial daughter," Patricia speaks through happy tears.

Drake just mutters something unintelligible in the background. "Like you would accept any addition in this family, mother, if it wasn't her; it was either Lily or no one."

I halt in the middle of wiping my tears away. "Patricia said that?" I look at my godmother, questioningly.

Patricia gracefully shrugs. "Something was up with you two in Mexico, but when we came back, I was surprised that Drake had gone back home and left you all alone in the villa. For eight years, we all wondered and watched as you two played hide-and-seek to avoid seeing each other. Your mom and I always wanted you and Drake to end up together. You two are perfect for each other. I can't understand for the life of me how you two don't see that. Of course, my brilliant son must've done something so irreparable for Lily to have ignored all of us, though."

Oh, were we that obvious? I hadn't realized.

"Mom, seriously, do we have to discuss this right now?" Drake starts to pace around the living room looking more stressed out.

My mom turns to me and uses that motherly tone, the one that says she won't take 'no comment' as an answer. "What happened in Mexico, Dear?"

Mom and Patricia look at me expectantly. I sigh and capitulate. "That night when you and Hugh left for Cozumel, I gave Drake my virginity. The next day, I woke up and he had left. When I tried to visit him in Columbia, he sent me an email stating that he's with someone, that it was serious and so forth. Of course, the rejection hurt me deeply because I had loved him for so long. I didn't want to date anyone when a lot of guys wanted to go out with me because I was saving myself for Drake. I didn't want anyone else. So when that happened, I realized that I was naïve and idiotic to believe that he would return my feelings. It obviously didn't mean anything to him so it was time to let it go. And I did. I realized that life does have more to offer than pining for someone who doesn't love you back. When Drake and I happened again, this time, it was all just sex. It was what we agreed upon and that's what it really was." Mom and Patricia's expressions are really hilarious. I would've laughed if this conversation wasn't as serious as it is.

I don't dare look in Drake's direction. I can feel him burning holes in me, but I don't have the capacity to look at the man who I once loved with all of my heart and my being.

"Oh dear, that was something I didn't expect, but I do understand why you don't want to marry Drake now. You two were in lust and are not in love. Marriage is only for people that are in love and that doesn't apply to you both. So, it's best that we just make the best of it and still be a family." My mom squeezes my hand in understanding.

Patricia on the other hand looks aghast. "How could you treat her so crassly, Drake? I knew you were a playboy, but I never in my life expected my son to treat a woman like a piece of meat, let alone take her virginity and then reject her the next day. I don't blame Lily at all for her decisions."

Drake swears and hastily leaves the room. We hear the front door slam one minute and his bike fires up the next. I sigh dejectedly. Had I known today was going to be a house of horrors, I would never have left the bed.

After the disastrous and taxing afternoon talk with Mom and Patricia, I decide to leave ten minutes later. I want to be alone and soothe my nerves, my mind and my heart.

When I get home, I immediately go out on my deck, trying to breathe and think rationally. I stay out and watch the sunset. I reject the idea of calling Masie. I don't want to hear 'I told you so' or better yet, 'give him another chance'. She will be as undecided as I am.

I still when there is a man walking towards me from afar. As he nears, I realize that it's Drake looking all rugged. The sunset hits the back of him and he looks too good to be true. When he reaches me, I see how his face is contorted, with what, I don't know. Pain? Sadness? Rejection?

"I figured you'd be out here, so I took a chance," he murmurs and sits on the other lounge chair next to me. "So, we're having a baby, huh? Do you want it? Our baby, I mean?" he rasps out, nervously.

"Of course, I want it. Since Dad died, I always felt like there's that big gaping hole in me that's missing. When I found out that I was pregnant, for the first time in years, I felt like I was going to be okay." I was a Daddy's girl and when he died so suddenly, I had a hard time dealing with it.

"I'm sorry about last night. You don't know how many times that situation has been shoved at me—even if it wasn't mine. It just came out of my mouth. I didn't sleep much because of it. I really am sorry." Drake does look remorseful, but too bad.

The damage is done.

"I meant what I said earlier, you don't need to feel obligated about parenting and such. I know you have a hectic lifestyle and I won't hold that against you. You have full visitation rights and we can work out something on weekends, if you choose to spend more time with the baby."

"Wow," Drake breathes out. "You thought this through that quickly? Did I mean so little to you?" His wounded pride and ego are not mine to save.

Life goes on. I had to realize that once when Drake broke me and I am determined to do it again. "The past doesn't matter. I'm concentrating on my future now."

Drake looks at me with profound hurt in his eyes. "How long did it take you to practice saying all that, Lil?"

Not long.

"I am done talking to you, Drake. I'm tired. I will have an ultrasound coming up. I will text you when and where. If you decide to join me, great; if not, I'll be fine on my own."

"Like hell I would miss seeing my child." Drake harrumphs and leaves me alone on my deck.

I feel bad that he's pissed off, but at the same time, Drake has handled everything so badly since he learned I was pregnant.

From asking me the paternity to blabbering it to my mother firsthand, he's done everything wrong. Yet, he doesn't seem to realize what he's doing to me—hurting me in the process which only makes me more resolved to not forgive him. If he can't even understand that he's doing things wrong, how can I hope for him to make things right?

22

We are in the hospital waiting area for our first ultrasound together and Drake looks anxious. He sighs for the umpteenth time and I grind my teeth together, irritated.

"If you sigh one more time I will murder you. For the love of God calm the heck down, will you?" I glare at him. Drake looks offended from my mild outburst.

"I get that you're hormonal and all, but don't bite my head off. I didn't do anything wrong. I'm just . . . I don't know, I guess I've never done this before," he murmurs, sullenly.

Wait, but wasn't Shannon pregnant before? "You didn't go with Shannon?"

He shakes his head. "She said it made her uncomfortable to have me in there with her. I had to do what I had to do to make her happy, I guess." What he spouts out next is completely unexpected. "I guess, now that I think about it, I'm not sure that she was pregnant to begin with. I think Shannon used that so I would marry her."

If I hadn't met the woman, I would argue about this, but I have and the woman is wretched, delusional and off her rocker. So, yes, I do agree with Drake on this score. "Good thing that you two didn't get hitched then. You should thank your lucky stars that I came in at the right moment and saved your sorry ass!"

Drake cocks his head and smiles at me. "Yeah, I do thank them . . . Every. Single. Day, Lil."

I wet my lips and look away. I suppose living with Shannon was one giant ball of nightmare. Yeah, he should be thanking those stars.

I'm more than thankful when they call out my name. We're ushered into a semi-dark room where the female doctor is kind enough to point out everything for us. Drake has tons of questions. The experience is definitely amazing. Our child is a puny thing on that screen, but I already love it with all of my heart.

After thirty minutes or so, we are driving back to my house. "That was totally crazy, don't you think?" Drake says much to himself, still amazed from the experience.

"Yeah, it was awesome to see it like that," I murmur. My thoughts are somewhere else.

I want to be detached from Drake, but he's making it impossible. I expect him to drop me off once we get to my house, but he follows me inside.

Since my plan was to ignore him, I go upstairs and shut my bedroom door. After a few minutes, I hear him knock.

"Lil?"

I groan. "What?"

"Can I come in?" he asks as he opens the door. "I just wanted to talk."

More talking, great. "Anything important?"

Drake pauses and sits on the foot of my bed. He waits a few more seconds before he starts, "Ever since the day we were born, we were meant for this. We were meant for each other, but it was my cowardice that made the journey a hell as I tried to fight it tooth and nail."

Damn, that admission from him hurts. He really doesn't want me. "Exactly, Drake, that's my point right there."

He huffs and gets up pacing, ending up leaning against the wall. "I was a total moron. It was a selfish thing to do, but at that age, it meant commitment and marriage would follow after you'd finished college. Our parents wouldn't have let us date without pushing us in that direction. I didn't want that. I wasn't ready for that, but I am now, Lily. If you just give me another chance. I do want you and the baby."

I sit up on the bed. "You are going to be a part of his or her life. I'm not going to take that from you."

"Yeah, but I want it all, with you included, as a family unit. Together."

Damn it. Fine. "I'll think about it. That's all I can tell you at the moment."

Drake comes over and kisses my forehead. "Thank you. I will work hard to earn your trust. I promise you that." He leaves after he gives me a beaming smile.

=====

I wake up the next day and find a note on the kitchen counter underneath a big vase of calla lilies along with a hearty breakfast of pancakes, bacon, eggs and a fruit bowl.

I just wanted to do something nice for you and the baby. I'll be thinking of you.

I smile like an idiot after reading it. I'm lucky enough that I don't have any morning sickness. Although I do get dizzy spells here and there, it isn't all that serious. I'll take dizzy spells anytime over vomiting my guts out.

From then on, I receive breakfast and different type of lilies on a daily basis. I spend most of my time reading baby books about what I should be expecting. Most days, I'm online checking out baby room designs and themes. Yeah, I'm ecstatic to be a mom and with Drake's breakfast redemption strategy, I am close to just getting over it and giving us both a fair shot.

After a week, I expect my day to go on like the usual, but something jolts me out of bed. I suppose it's my growling tummy or just my senses are piqued . . .

In my soft cotton night dress, I groggily make my way downstairs, yawning. I pause when I see Drake in the kitchen cooking. When he feels my presence, he smiles and greets me. "Good morning, Baby Momma. Hungry?"

Very much, yes, I'm so hungry for you. He looks so delicious whistling and cooking in my kitchen, I want him for breakfast. Instead, my sanity snaps me back from dreamland and pushes me forward to get some juice.

"Just go sit. I've got you covered. Today's your day to be lazy. I'm at your service." He points at my breakfast nook and quickly places a glass of orange juice on the table.

"Thank you." When I take a refreshing sip, I notice that it's fresh squeezed juice. "This is delicious. Where did you buy this?" I want to get more.

"I bought the oranges at Whole Foods, but squeezed them myself. You have more in the fridge, Babe."

I blink a few times. The thought of Drake squeezing oranges makes me hornier than I was originally. What is wrong with me today? I'm just a huge hornball. "Thanks. That's very thoughtful of you," I thank him, though I'm a little uncomfortable about where my thoughts are leading.

Drake places pancakes, a Mexican omelet, fresh honey dew slices and strawberries before me. He then slides in the opposite side of the table, folding his arms and looks at me. "You know I'd do anything for you, right? Now go eat and feed my baby, woman."

I smile and chuck a strawberry at him—which he catches and sexily bites into. The pink juices of the fruit sit deliciously on his lips. *Honey drops,* I think as my eyes glue on to them, hungrily. When his tongue juts out and licks the residue, I bite my bottom lip to stop myself from moaning at the very sight of his pink tongue snaking out. I imagine all sorts of naughty things accompanying that tongue of his.

Drake groans and gets up from his seat. "Come here," he throatily whispers. When I get close to him, he kisses me passionately and I have a hard time breathing in between his kisses.

It doesn't take long for me to hook my arms around his neck, and when he lifts me up and places me on top of the table, his hands hastily push the dishes aside. Biting his bottom lip, my hands seek out the edge of his shirt and pull it out of his pants. The sight of his hard-toned body sends me into a delicious, sexual hysteric.

"I want you," I whisper against his left nipple before my tongue licks it and my teeth bite into it. Drake hisses as his hands reach out for my thin night wear and swiftly pulls it off my body. My stomach is still fairly flat, but you can faintly see a slight bump if you stare hard enough.

Drake steps back a little bit as his eyes voraciously caress my body in burningly from my toes up. "God, you're beautiful."

Our eyes connect; his are full of desire and mine are desperate. He takes a step forward and seizes my lips again, but this time, I have no intention of stopping. My hands immediately go to his jeans and unlatch them. I pull down his underwear with his pants in an instant as I greedily capture his hot length.

"Shit, slow down," Drake hisses.

No way, Jose, not in this lifetime, I think lasciviously.

When my grip goes tighter around him, Drake shifts the power and takes charge. He has me out of my panties in a heartbeat. I barely have time to blink before his fingers delve inside my wet folds. Being pregnant makes everything so sensitized and arousing. Each stroke takes me a step closer to Nirvana. I can't hold back what my body wants and

I want everything from him. I plant my hands behind me as I lean backwards. His other hand spreads my legs wider while I watch Drake's tongue descend on me while his silver eyes have me suspended.

Everything becomes hazy after that as Drake makes love to me all day long.

=====

"Drake, will you call me back? You said you wanted to go to the movies. If you've changed your mind then say so! You're over an hour late. You know what? Forget it. I'd rather stay home because I am that angry. Yes, so angry in fact, I could murder you right now. Bye." I huff again and plop down on my couch.

It is already six-thirty when my stomach growls in protest. I get up and head to the kitchen to prepare a chicken sandwich. I'm halfway through my meal when I hear Mom knock and enter my home. "Lily?"

"I'm in the kitchen, Mom." I gulp down half of my apple juice when she strides towards me. I'm instantly caught off guard when my mom doesn't have a sunny smile to greet me. Instead, she looks worried and teary.

I still. My mind is going into panic mode and my heart pounds madly against my ribcage. "Mom? What's going on?" I whisper when I watch her halt midway.

She starts crying. The sight of her crying makes me frightened and worried. Whatever this is, it's serious. I rush to her side and try to calm her.

"Baby, I'm so sorry." Mom starts sobbing even harder.

Sorry for what? "What about, Mom? Please, you're killing me here. Tell me."

"Pat and Hugh just got a call thirty minutes ago telling them that Drake was in an eight-car accident. He's in the hospital right now, but it doesn't look too good."

I let go of her as I stare at her in disbelief. "No. No. We were supposed to go watch movies tonight. I was waiting for him . . ." I trail off as the horror of what she told me hits me as I watch her cry some more.

Drake . . . in an accident . . . doesn't look too good. Meaning he could die . . . his chances aren't too good.

Tears gather in my eyes as I drop to the floor holding my stomach. What do I do if he dies? What about our baby? Our baby will grow up without a father. A life without Drake . . . I won't accept it. Drake has to fight to get better. He can't leave me here alone and pregnant.

Shaking, I speak. "Mom, do you mind taking me to him? I need to see him."

My mom nods and guides me out the door. Everything is a blur until we get outside the hospital. Then, it becomes all too clear to me. Drake is inside, possibly dying. I'm a wreck when Mom and I reach Patricia and Hugh in the waiting room right outside the OR. Both of them come to me and hug me tightly. Patricia is sobbing uncontrollably. Hugh is tearing up.

"He's in the operating room right now. He hit his head pretty badly during impact. There was some bleeding on his brain and a broken knee. The doctor said he'll let us know if there is any update," Hugh says through tears.

Mom helps me to the nearest chair and all four of us sit there vigilantly while we listen to Patricia cry.

"Please don't take my baby from me," Patricia keeps muttering and praying.

I get up then and decide to seek out the hospital Chapel. When Mom offers to come, I decline. I want to be alone.

As I sit on one of the wooden benches, I feel the eerie peace greet me. The Crucifix situated before has two tiny lights focused on it. As I look at it, I feel sadness wash over me.

I remember the last time I prayed desperately. That was when Dad was in the operating room. Dad had stage-four liver cancer. At that point, the doctor was telling us that he might not survive it and that we should prepare ourselves for the operation possibly not being successful. However, I was hopeful. My father was a robust man and a stubborn one. He skipped his doctor's appointment and purposely missed his colonoscopy. Since he was a busy man, he thought that his daily intake of vitamins was his magic pill and nothing could ever touch him. Let alone a cancer. He was wrong, though. The cancer got to him all because he wanted to be oblivious to what was going on with his body.

If he had just addressed what he was feeling, then instead of shrugging and brushing it off, he might have had a chance to survive. I suppose, in some ways, we are our own worst enemy.

If I pray, will God grant me my prayer?

On my knees on the cushioned pedestal, I place my arms on the back of the wooded panel before me and clasp my hands. Closing my eyes, I pray.

"If you can grant me a wish, will you hear me this time? All my life, I pray only when it's needed, but that doesn't mean I don't believe in you. Since Dad died, I've been bitter and I don't want to be that person anymore. This baby is a miracle. I feel alive again, but it seems that it will come with a high price in exchange for Drake's life. I beg you don't make me have this baby alone. My baby needs its father. Give Drake and me a chance to be parents together. Give me a chance to tell him that I love him. I have never stopped and I don't think I ever will. Drake took my heart and left with it. He never gave it back. Give me an even shot at happiness because without him, I don't know what I'll do. Help me. Please, help me. I need you to help me . . . Hear me, at least."

Wiping my tears away, I sit back down again and hold my belly. "Your daddy's fighting for his life right now. Let's be strong for him," I murmur to my belly.

I don't know how long I sit there, staring blindly. I don't even hear Mom come in.

"Lil, maybe it's time to go home? You need to rest for the baby. You've been in here for two hours."

Two hours? I've been staring for two hours?

I nod to my mom. "Let me just say goodbye to Patricia and Hugh. Maybe they have news about Drake."

Mom holds me with one arm as we walk the white halls of the hospital. The intercoms are paging doctors, the beeping sounds of machines surround us, the hushed whispers and the crying relatives are the ambient background noise to the symphony about sickness and death.

My feet feel heavy, but I make it to the elevator. When we get out, I notice a doctor speaking to a family in a hushed solemn manner. I halt when I hear the woman scream.

"Noooooooooo! No! No! There's got to be a way. You have to save my son! He's only seventeen."

I stand frozen as her screams and pleas are all being hushed down by her surrounding family. The daunting voices inside my head start again.

God, that voicemail I left him . . . I feel sick just thinking about it. Tears fall freely on my face. Drake . . . I'm so sorry. I feel like I've let him down because of my own selfishness and holding on to the past, I have let us down and our baby.

What if it's too late now? What if he doesn't survive and dies on that operating table? My breathing becomes ragged as my thoughts move to picturing him on that table being cut open. His body pale and lifeless and there is nothing I can do to help him live.

Sobs rock through me as I sense my entire body start to feel weird and heavy. The last thing I remember is the airy light feel of my body falling before I black out.

23

I groan and feel my mom soothing me. It takes a good minute to remember all the events that have happened. Drake.

"How's Drake? Where is he?"

"He's in the ICU, Dear. He's still not in the clear and they still consider him in critical condition. The doctor said to wait a few days for everything to heal and see if the surgery worked."

When I try to move my hand and my heavy lids finally open, I realize that I'm in a hospital bed with a hospital gown on. "Mom?" I look at her questioningly. "What happened?"

"You passed out. Thank God I caught you before you hit your head on the floor. The doctor said that this sometimes happens when pregnant women are stressed out. You should stay put until the doctor says it's okay for you to be discharged." Mom looks at me worriedly, misty-eyed.

"Sorry, Mom. I didn't mean to scare you." The last thing my mom needs right now is to worry about my pregnant state as well. All of us are going through so much; I can't afford to have the rest of them worry about me when Drake's life is still on the line.

Even though it kills me to resign and rest, instead of going upstairs to be with Drake, I force myself to stay put. For Drake and the baby; I can do it for them.

=====

The next day, when the doctor, whose name I don't care to remember, clears me to go home, I immediately go to see Drake in ICU.

Drake being placed in the ICU speaks volumes about how serious his condition is, but I have to be strong. I need to see him. I have to or I will go crazy.

When we get to the private lounge, Hugh and Patricia look worse for wear. It takes me about ten minutes to convince all of them to go home and get some rest. I want to be alone when I see him. I want to spend time with him.

I still myself before I enter his room. I'm not prepared to see the state that he is in.

Drake has tubes around his mouth, his head is wrapped with a bandage and his complexion is pale and ashen. I sag against the closed door frame as I watch the up and down bleeping of the monitor and his breathing ventilator as that too, eerily moves up and down. My tears instantly pool in my eyes as I slowly walk towards his bed.

"Drake," I whisper chokingly as I reach for his lifeless hand. I stroke it lightly, hating the cold feel of it. "It's Lily. If you can hear me, I beg you, don't leave me like this." I wipe the tears that fall down my face. I want to say more, but I start to bawl hard.

I think I hate myself more for being so selfish with him the last couple of weeks. All that wasted time, for what? Because I was hurt before? Now that there's a big possibility of him dying, I don't think I can forgive myself for wasting the precious time that I could've spent in his arms because I was being selfish.

I clutch his hand, hard. My heart lurches when I hear an alarming sound.

The sound of death.

It's the flat line sound of the heart monitor. It takes me a good second to realize what's going on.

With hot tears in my eyes, I stare at his hand, and then back to the monitor. Then, I scream for help. I know the nurses were alerted the second his monitor went flat, but I'm not prepared for the commotion that rattles into the room. Six nurses and a male doctor come in with a rush. The doctor is barking frantic orders as the Defibrillator is being prepped for use. They open his gown at his chest and place a good amount of gel before the doctor uses the paddles to attempt to resuscitate Drake back to life.

I'm against the cold hospital wall as I watched it all in horror. I think half of me dies when the doctor yells, "Clear."

I close my eyes as my tears fall down my face. I pray, drowning the rushed scuttle of their voices and movements, not wanting to hear any of it as they try to bring his lifeless body back to life.

"Please, please! Hear me. Give Drake his life back. Don't take him from me. I love him. Please . . . Hear me . . ."

I tense when I feel a strong hand on my arm. "Mrs. Tatum?" I don't even think to correct him that I'm not Mrs. Tatum because I wish I was now.

My misty eyes flutter open and connect to the worried face of the doctor. How I wish I was now. Fuck! My stomach drops.

"No! NO! NO!" I scream and fall on the floor when my legs give out.

The doctor and a couple nurses help me into the chair. "He's alive. We managed to bring him back. The nurses will be back to check again with his progress and get more scans from him." I merely nod in my dazed state.

When they've all left, I stare at Drake's body. I'm scared to reach out and touch him, just in case he dies again. I don't think I could endure it if he dies when I touch him a second time. So, I stay in my seat, on edge. After an hour of nurses going in and out of the room, they wheel him out to get CT scans. I didn't realize I fell asleep until a stranger's voice wakes me.

"Miss Lily?"

I blink a few times before I focus on the warm smile of the nurse before me. When she sees my questioning look, she smiles wider. "He's awake. He's been asking for you."

I suddenly stand up and look over. When the nurse leaves, I slowly walk over to the bed.

"Drake?" I shakily whisper his name.

Drake slowly turns his head, groaning. "Lil," he mumbles without opening his eyes.

He's really awake! My Drake is awake!

In that instant, I go and cry on his chest. Bawling and howling my sorrows. "God, I'm so sorry for being so awful. I'm sorry." I slowly lift my upper body, scolding myself for being stupid. His chest is probably hurting after what it has gone through, my heavy head doesn't need to add to the problem.

"Shhh, don't cry, Babe." Drake slowly lifts his eyelids, his eyes a little glazed over.

"I'm sorry." I sniff and give him a smile.

His weak hand reaches out to me and cups my face as he slowly wipes my tears away. I close my eyes, loving the brush of his hand on me. "I love you, Lil. It was the only thing I could think about before the car crashed. I was thinking that I didn't get the chance to tell you how much I love you." His voice is paper-thin and hoarse.

I hold his hand against my face and kiss it. "I love you, Drake. I have never stopped loving you. When I spoke those words eight years ago, I meant them. It hasn't changed."

He gives me a weak smile before he closes his eyes. "Stay with me, please? I want you close." Drake lightly coughs, his breathing ragged.

I wouldn't dare move even if the President asked it of me. "Always. I will be here, next to you." I pull a chair up and place it next to his bed. I hold his hand the whole time while I watch him breathe in and out.

Once in a while, Drake squeezes my hand, but keeps his eyes shut. I bet the drugs they gave him are powerful. Whatever helps him rest and heal.

Emotionally exhausted and pregnant, it doesn't take long for me to fall asleep with his hand against my cheek.

24

"Sweetie, you have to eat something." Patricia urges me to eat the lunch they brought in.

All three scrambled back here when they were informed about what happened with Drake. Hugh and my mom are at the connecting private lounge, but I stick next to Drake because I promised that I would stay close and because I don't want to be anywhere else. My place is with him. It always has been. It was only a matter of time until he and I realized that.

"Do you mind just bringing the food in here with me? I don't want to leave his side." Patricia smiles sadly at me. Dark circles and frown lines that were not there a few days ago are now evident on her beautiful face.

"I will sit with my son and wait until you are done. Please, you're pregnant. You can't risk both of your lives as well.

With difficultly, I finally let go of Drake's hand and get up from my chair. Patricia takes my seat. I hear her speaking softly to her son before I leave the room, exhausted.

"Hugh just stepped out to take care of some business. I have your prenatal vitamins and some other stuff that you need." Mom gives me the much needed vitamins. I down one with a bottled orange juice.

When she presents me with a gourmet sandwich, I barely manage to swallow the tiny bites I make, but I do, for the baby. I don't even care how the food tastes. Everything is automated. I just want to get it over with so that I can go back to Drake.

"How are you feeling?" my mother asks. I'm sure she is referring to the scary shock of my life earlier when Drake died for a few minutes.

I stare at the bottled juice that sits on the table before me. How am I feeling? I feel like I've been dragged to Hell and back. There are no words to describe how I am feeling. The man I love died for a few minutes. Where do I even begin with all of that?

After a few minutes of just staring into space while flashbacks run through my head, I finally look at my mom and see that she has tears in her eyes. "Thank you for being here. I love you."

Mom comes over and gives me a tight hug, sniffing. "Be strong. Drake will recover. He's young and he's a stubborn man at that."

I cry in her arms. My mother's smell and comfort give me strength and new found bravery. If there is another person who understands what I'm going through, it's my mom. Before my father died, she held it together even though the pain was written all over her face. I cry until I had no more tears left. When I come up for air, she urges me to wash my face before returning to sit next to Drake. "You'll feel better when you freshen up, trust me."

And it does help. Not a whole lot, but it helps me feel a little lighter inside.

=====

It's around three in the afternoon when the doctor comes into the room. He introduces himself as Dr. Readings. He's a man in his late fifties with salt and pepper hair, kind eyes and a warm sympathetic smile.

He faces Patricia and Hugh before he speaks. "We found several blood clots in Drake. They're travelling upwards and we want to operate quickly before it turns into a pulmonary embolism. If it reaches his lungs before we get to it, his chances of survival are slim."

Is he serious? Hasn't Drake gone through enough? Another surgery? What if that will cause an infection or another complication, what then?

Patricia body starts to shake and she sags in the chair. Watching how his wife looks like she has lost a battle, Hugh takes charge. "When can you schedule the operation? I want it done as soon as possible. I think we can all agree that my only son has gone through Hell for the last two days. Do what you have to do. I expect to have the best of the best on the operating team for my son. Do you have recommendations for doctors to be flown in?"

"I can actually recommend another doctor to operate with me. I am highly qualified, but I want another qualified doctor in there with me. I will give him a call right away and hopefully we can schedule it later this evening. I will get back to you shortly." The doctor excuses himself before Patricia and Mom start crying again.

Another operation.

How the hell am I going to survive another one?

Fuck! When it rains, it really pours, hard, with no concession.

After an hour, the doctor confirms that the specialist is on board and should be here around six that night. The emergency operation is scheduled for seven.

I feel like a crying zombie.

My eyes just keep weeping and there's no stopping it. The well of tears doesn't stop while I sit next to Drake's sleeping body.

My head falls flat on the bed, exhausted. I'm pleasantly woken up with soft, gentle strokes on my cheek. My face feels crusty after crying.

"Hey . . . you're crying again," I hear Drake whisper sadly.

Still sleepy, I manage to lift my head and meet his silver eyes. "I can't help it."

Drake tries to give me a reassuring smile, but fails miserably. "They're going to wheel me out in twenty minutes to prep me for the operation."

I still. Damn, I slept for hours! Fuck!

Drake's throat bobs a few times before his hoarse voice gives me infinite dread. I start to shiver. "Just in case I don't survive—" he starts, but I cover his dry lips with my fingers, hushing him.

"No. Don't think like that. You will survive this. You're a fighter. Don't give up on me . . . or the baby. Please," I beg. I watch as his face contorts with pain.

"I will try, Lil. You know I will, but this is beyond my control." He reaches for my hand and lightly tugs me closer to place my head on his chest. When he speaks again, he's choked up with tears, too. "I don't want to die. I want to see you swell with my baby. I want to see my child being born into this world. I want to share that joy with you. I wish that more than anything. You must believe me." His voice shakes and it takes him another minute to speak again while I listen to his erratic heartbeat.

"If things turn for the worst, I'm hoping you will name our child with my last name? I want him or her to have something of me."

My body racks with sobs. The thought of Drake thinking about this breaks my heart. It simply, fucking, breaks me into pieces.

"When the time comes, I want you to move on. I want my child to have a good loving home and a good father figure for him or her. Will you . . . promise me that, Lil?"

How can I promise him something so repulsive? I don't want anyone else. I want him.

Drake.

No one else.

I lift my face off his chest and look at the man whose fighting spirit is non-existent. "No. I won't promise you that. I will never fucking promise you that, Drake Tatum. There will be no other man, except you, do you hear me? So, get your ass in gear because you will survive this. You can and you will do this because if you don't, I will fucking die without you. Do you hear me? Yeah, I will die from heartache. So, please, don't do that to me." My chest aches and contracts when I speak those words to him. I mean each and every one of them.

That definitely shut his 'move on after I die' speech. He even manages to laugh, though it sounds like it is a lot of struggle to do so. At least he's smiling again. "Damn, you are right, woman. I forgot how stubborn you are." His eyes trace my face, studying me with great intensity. "I've always loved you. I think I fell in love with you after we did that fake marriage in the gazebo. I'm sorry I fought against it. I was stupid and young."

"I knew you set me up for a good reason." I laugh. Our laughter is short lived when the nurses come and inform us that it's time for Drake to go to the OR.

We hold hands as they slowly wheel him out of the room. Once we get to the OR, the nurse informs us that this is the furthest that I can go. My heart dreads and aches as I watch Drake say his goodbyes to his parents. My mom hugs him fiercely before leaving me to talk to Drake.

I give him a chaste kiss on the lips. "I will see you very soon. Think of me and our future together while you're dreaming, okay? I love you, Drake."

That seems to put him in good spirits. Good. We need all the help we can get to make him fight inside the operating room. "I will see you very soon. I love you, Babe."

I give him another kiss before the nurse takes him away from me. I stare at the door and pray to God that he will bring Drake back to me.

There's nothing I can do, but hope for the best.

25

We vigilantly wait for hours on end and don't leave the waiting room area until we hear news from the doctors inside.

The waiting part is the worst battle anyone can be faced with.

We almost jump in our seats when the doctor approaches us.

"The operation was a success. He's doing fine, but he's still not in the clear. He should be out very soon."

He's about to leave, but I stop him. "Wait! What do you mean exactly by 'he's still not in the clear'?"

"That there are still a lot of possibilities for him to have complications."

I merely nod my head before he leaves us and goes back inside the OR. Fear grips me, making it hard for me to breathe.

"Sit down, Lil, and try to relax. He should be out soon." Mom tries to calm me down as she guides me back to my seat.

After over an hour, Drake is finally back in his private room looking as pale as ever. I'm alone in the room, the rest are out in the connected private sitting room. I stand at the foot of the bed, staring at him, scared and helpless.

When I glance back at the monitor, I notice that the digits are starting to decline. "Mom?"

"Mom!!!" I scream.

"What? What's wrong?" Hugh comes inside. He glances at the monitor when it starts to beep.

"No, not again!" Hugh panics, but manages to call for the nurse.

Mom and Patricia start to look frightened. When the nurse comes and reassures us that it's normal for the blood pressure to drop after a surgery, it doesn't help ease my worries.

The nurse then checks for dehydration and whatever else that is needed. I watch it all, still stuck at the foot of the bed.

"Lily! You're bleeding!" Patricia yells, horrified as she looks at my blood stained jeans.

The blood is seeping through my jeans quickly. I look up at them, powerless. "What's happening?" I whisper. Tears start to form in my eyes, blurring everything.

That's the last thing I say before everything goes black, darkness takes me in.

=====

When I wake up the next day, Mom and Colin are in the room with me. Mom is silently crying while Colin tries to soothe her.

"The baby?" I croak out. It's the first thing that enters my brain when I wake up.

Mom sadly shakes her head, tearing up again.

My throat constricts, but I swallow back the tears. I can't fall apart now, Drake is still in danger. "Drake?"

"He's fine. He's stable now," Colin manages to respond because Mom is still crying.

"Can you guys take me home? I want to be alone."

"The doctor advises that you stay the night, so they can monitor you," Colin says with worry, knowing where my thoughts are heading.

"I'll rest at home. I promise, I will. I want to be discharged, please? I need to be alone, please," I beg them both.

"Is that what you really want, Sweetie?" Mom asks, understanding my need to be alone.

I give her a small nod. "Yes."

"Okay," Mom whispers before she gets up to take care of it.

Half an hour later, Colin and Mom are driving me home. I declined when they asked me if I wanted to visit Drake before I left. I couldn't handle it.

Not in the state that I'm in, not without having a nervous breakdown.

When Colin parks outside my house, I tell him to stay in the car. Mom helps me out and walks me to the door. "I can take it from here, Mom. Tell Pat and Hugh I will be there in a day or two."

Mom hugs me. "I love you. I want to be here for you, but it seems that you need to be on your own. I don't agree with this, but I am going to respect your need for privacy. I'm a phone call away," she reminds me.

"I love you, too," I whisper, trying to hold it together.

She waits for me to get in the house before she turns and leaves with Colin.

I don't bother turning on the lights. The darkness suits my feeling and my mood. It's odd when I walk. There is this weird hollowness in my stomach. There's only a hint of pain to remind me that I lost something today.

I feel completely empty.

When I get upstairs, instead of going directly into my bedroom, I go across the hall to the other room. I stand against the door, my hand gripping the handle. I slowly open it and go inside.

That very same day when Drake got into the car accident, I spent all morning painting and rearranging the small bedroom. Taking out things that weren't needed, so I would have space for a crib, a diaper changing station, a rocking chair; the things I had ordered online that day.

The eggshell colored paintjob is only halfway done; I remember thinking that I would have all the next day to finish it.

There it was, unfinished. Just like my pregnancy.

I wanted that baby. I was excited to have something to look forward to, but it was short-lived.

A dying scream comes from me before I curl up on the floor, sobbing uncontrollably.

I'm crying for my dad. For Drake.

But most of all, I cry for the baby I never got the chance to know, to hold. The baby I loved will just be in my memory. Forever stuck there, frozen.

26

The next day, I wake still curled up on the floor. I slowly stand and go inside my bedroom to cry more in bed.

I need to cry it out before I head back to the hospital tomorrow. If Drake wakes up and sees me in a terrible state, I don't want him to blame himself.

He'd think it was his fault that I lost the baby, but I know it is mine. I was negligent. I barely ate; especially, with the stress level I was going through with Drake. I was advised to take proper nutrition and hydrate all the time, but I didn't. It's my fault that I lost my baby.

When I wake the following morning, Mom is downstairs cooking me breakfast. "Good morning. Drake's awake. I came by to make sure you're doing fine and to tell you the news."

I feel relief, but not enough to dull the pain inside me. The hollowness hasn't left me. "I will be going out to see him later."

Mom plants a plate before me, mushroom and cheese omelet with a glass of orange juice. She then kisses my forehead and whispers, "Stay strong. There's no one to blame. Sometimes life has its own way of dealing with things. I'm sorry you have to go through this, though. Do you want to talk about it?"

My chest feels heavy. Each breath I take hurts. "No, I need time to cope with it first. Don't tell Drake anything yet."

"We know. It isn't our place to tell him that. Whenever you're ready, then you can do that yourself."

I silently eat my breakfast. I'm not hungry, but I force it down, anyway.

Mom waits until I'm ready to head back to the hospital. I'm relieved to find Drake sleeping when I get there.

After an hour, he wakes, asking for me. "Where's Lily?"

I get up and get my crap together. "Hey, nice to finally see you up and awake." I smile at him as I walk towards his bed.

He groggily smiles at me, reaching for my hand. I clasp it with mine, needing assurance, needing his love and his warmth. "I made it," Drake whispers happily.

I wipe the tears running down my face. "You did. Thank you for that. I wouldn't have forgiven you if you didn't."

"Don't cry. I'll get better, I promise. I'll be as good as new when our baby comes." Drake slowly reaches out and softly wipes my tears away.

Not knowing what to say, I simply nod.

"I'm tired, but I want you to stay close. I love knowing that you're here, holding my hand," he whispers before his eyes start to close.

"I'll be here. I promise."

A small smile forms on his lips, eyes still shut. "I love you," he manages to whisper. I know he's asleep when his grip softens.

I sit next to him, kissing his hand and telling him how much I love him, too.

=====

Drake isn't allowed to go home for two weeks.

In those two weeks, I entertain him with board games, reading and watching movies. Drake slowly regains his strength. I have successfully dodged all of his questions about the baby, answering them vaguely.

It works, for a bit, but the day before he's to be discharged, he asks again.

I come into his room around ten in the morning with breakfast in hand. "Good morning! Did you sleep well?" I ask.

"I did, thanks. Now, come over here and give me a kiss." I laugh at his demand. Apart from the bandage around his head, Drake looks almost like his old self. I bend over and give him a kiss. I expect it to be quick, but I'm surprised when he takes hold of my head and devours my lips. Kissing me so passionately, it breaks my heart. When he lets go of me, I'm out of breath. We both pant as we stare at each other.

"I've been meaning to do that. I wanted to wait until we were home, but you came in here looking so beautiful, I couldn't help it." Drake holds my hand and plants a kiss on it.

"I've missed you, too."

We eat breakfast as we watch CNN. "You're twelve weeks today, right? What time is your appointment?" he inquires while his attention turns back to the television screen.

I still, slowly placing the food back on the plate. "About that . . . there's . . . there's no more baby, Drake. I lost it."

Drake suddenly looks at me, confused. "What do you mean? When?" The shock comes first, then the pain surfaces on his face.

"Just after you came out of surgery the second time, I started to bleed." I feel wretched for not telling him immediately, but there was so much going on, it was hard for me to do it.

"Are you okay? God, all this time . . . you're smiling and making me laugh . . . when you were probably dying inside."

I was.

Still am.

"I'm still reeling from it. Being with you makes me feel happy, though. I'm sorry it took me so long to tell you, but it was hard to talk about it, still is." I get choked up, but I push it down.

"Don't be sorry. I'm the one who's sorry. We wouldn't be here if it weren't for me." I shake my head, denying it. "I'm here, Babe. We'll go through this together. I don't want you to think that you're all alone in this. I don't ever want you to feel that way."

I never did doubt it. "I know you're here for me, Drake."

=====

"How does it feel to be back home?" I ask as we enter his foyer.

Skull comes out running to greet his owner. He's been under the care of Drake's housekeeper who was kind enough to stay with him for the last two weeks.

"Hey, Buddy! Did you miss me?" Drake scratches the dog's neck.

"Are you tired? You should rest. If you're hungry, I can cook up something," I ask when we are going up the stairs, heading towards his bedroom.

"I think I'm going to crash for a bit. I'm exhausted."

I'm shocked to find his room has had a major transformation. The décor, the bed and everything else is different.

Seeing my expression, Drake explains, "I hired an interior decorator to strip everything off. The bathrooms, the closets and the rest of the guestrooms are all newly decorated. After Shannon, I thought it was best to change everything to make you feel comfortable."

Could he be any sweeter?

"Thank you. This means so much to me, Drake." I stride towards where he stands and give him a kiss.

"Stay with me in bed. I want you close." Drake looks tired. If he wants me next to him, then I'll be right there.

Once we are all in bed, Skull included, I ask, "Why do you always want me close to you? Each time you ask it, your voice changes. It's weird."

"I had a dream . . . I died in it. When you learned of the news, you were so devastated; you wouldn't stop crying. Then my dreams flashed forward and you were with Jared with my child growing in your belly."

"I'm not going to leave you for him. You know that, don't you?"

"I do, but when I'm reminded of how helpless I was in my dream, how badly I wanted to be that man for you and I couldn't because I was dead, I feel raw, and you being close gives me a reality check; that you're here with me and that I'm still alive. I don't want to ever feel that kind of pain, Lil. It scares me to think that it could easily happen." Drake sounds vulnerable, gutted.

I snuggle close to him, resting my head on his arm since I can't put my head on his chest, yet. "That will never happen because I'm not capable of loving another man. The last eight years taught me that." It wasn't because of my luck of trying. I did try, very hard, but it was impossible when I'd given my heart away already.

"It was always you in my heart, Lil. I'm happy that you're here, still giving me another chance after how I treated you. For loving me as I am."

We hold hands as we both fall asleep; the strain of the past couple of weeks finally catching up with me.

27

I wake the next morning feeling refreshed and upbeat. Drake is still asleep when I get out of bed and hunt down something to change into.

His closet is completely new. The thought of it makes me smile. He really did think of me. I didn't even have to tell him that the feeling of Shannon was all over the house, making me feel uncomfortable. He had just known. I choose his Columbia shirt and go inside the bathroom to shower. I completely forgot to pack a bag before I left my house yesterday.

The new fitted bathroom is made of black marble and a lot of glass and mirrors. The total opposite of the all-white and chrome theme he had before.

After my quick shower, I wear his shirt over my naked body. When I get out and stride past the bed, Drake is still asleep.

I head downstairs and make breakfast. I'm flipping pancakes when Drake appears in the kitchen. Fresh out of the shower, bandage gone, and wearing a black shirt with navy blue sweats.

My stupid body reacts to him instantly. "Did the doctor say it was okay to take the bandage off?" I ask, trying to distract myself while I start to make coffee.

"He did." Drake comes over and hugs me from behind. "Good morning," he whispers, sniffing my neck. "You look good in my shirt."

"I forgot to bring my clothes," I mumble, my body weak against him.

"I don't mind. You look sexy. I don't mind seeing you wearing my shirt every day." Drake slowly spins me around to face him.

With a finger, he slowly lifts my chin to meet his metallic gaze. He looks unreadable.

His eyes probe inside me, reaching until it holds something.

My soul. My heart.

"Marry me."

I press my lips together as his words settle in. "Are you sure? You're not doing this because of that dream, right? I'm not going anywhere. You don't have to propose marriage to make sure I'm going to stick around."

His eyes never leave mine. They are serious, bold and undaunted. "That, too, but I've wanted to ask you for a long time. I wanted to ask you that first night you spent here, but the thought of you rejecting me was something I couldn't deal with then. I'm asking you now because the thought of spending even a day without you seems too much. I love you . . . but I would give anything to love you as my wife."

Ah, hell. My tears start flowing again. I'm laughing and crying at the same time. He starts to laugh with me as he wipes the tears away. "Damn it, Drake. How the hell do you expect me to decline a proposal like that? Yes, yes, yes! I will marry you."

"Yeah? Are you sure?" Drake asks as he gently kisses me.

"Like you would give me a chance to decline you." My arms circle around his neck.

"Damn right, woman. I will hound you on a daily basis if I have to. You will never be free of me."

I pull back a little, just enough for us to gaze into each other's eyes. Drake . . . I have always loved you . . . always . . . "I promise to give you kisses and share my Reese's peanut buttercups once a week for forever and ever until I die."

He opens his mouth and laughs. "God, Babe, after all these years, you remembered."

Blushing, I lovingly kiss his cheek. "You bet your ass, I remember. It was my wedding day. I cherished it. Don't you remember it? Any of it?"

Drake looks serious all of a sudden. "I remember. It's not something I could forget, either. Instead of telling you, however, I want to show you instead."

"But your doctor . . ." I trail off as his hand cups my womanhood.

"Good God. You were planning to eat breakfast with me like this? Are you trying to kill me?" I moan his name as he starts to rub me. "Always so wet for me, aren't you?"

"Yes, but you have to stop." As much as I'm tempted to make love to him, I'm not sure if it's safe to do so.

"Not in this lifetime, my wife. Not in this motherfucking lifetime."

My wife.

I can't argue much about that as Drake sticks a finger inside me and both of our hunger grows out of control.

EPILOGUE

Three months later

Drake

"How are you feeling tonight, married and all?" I murmur, stroking Lily's hair. I hear her blissfully sigh against my chest.

We are wrapped in each other's arms as we look towards the sky, loving the soft breeze of the Caribbean Sea.

We went back to where it all began. I was persistent that we spend our honeymoon here. I didn't want to go anywhere else. This place meant something to me. It was the place where I realized that I was very much in love with the woman in my arms. But most importantly, this place also evoked painful memories for her. I wanted to change that because from here on out, I was hell-bent on giving her good, beautiful memories. Although, I'm not deluded that there will be challenges along the way, but I truly believe that with her by my side, we can overcome anything life throws at us.

Only five hours ago, we said our vows amongst our friends and family in a small Chapel in Santa Monica. I belonged with Lily, and she with me. Each time I remember how it felt to lose her the second time, I admit, it still gripped me with a great sense of loss of death. It really felt that way when she wouldn't take me back. There was no room for another colossal mistake. I was given another chance at life, and I was going to spend the rest of it showing and loving the woman who had me from the start.

"I love being married to you," Lily says as she kisses the healing scar on my chest.

"You have no idea how much I love being your husband, woman." I roll her onto her back and hover above her, gazing down at the most beautiful woman who held my heart captive. She simply gives me a smile.

A smile that shows me her unconditional love.

I know the accident brought everything into perspective. Though it was a scary situation to be that close at the death's door, I couldn't help but feel grateful that it happened because it brought us together. I love Lily with everything that I am and all that I could ever be, as a man, a lover, a husband, and hopefully a father, later on.

During our flight, we agreed and decided that it was best to wait a year or two before we try to have a baby. To this day, each time we brought up the subject about our lost child, it still brought a violent ache in my chest. We both still feel the massive loss, but we take comfort at the thought that we will make one down the line. Since we are both an only child, I want four children.

Does she agree?

I suppose you could say that a man needs to hone his negotiating skills more when it comes to his new wife. But right now, I am more than happy to settle and just enjoy us together. It seems that we are both eager to spend more time getting to know each other again. And let me just say that, it has been the best months of my life.

I roll to my side and start to kiss the swell of her breasts. She moans my name as I brush my hungry lips against her sensitive ear.

"Stars, Babe. I want you to see those fucking stars." I was not going to let up until she was bursting with millions of them when I take her through waves after waves of orgasms.

Married life, I was definitely driven to make ours perfect.

The End